The Tongue I Dream In

Sheree Renée Thomas

PM PRESS | 2026

“The Tongue We Dream In” first appeared in *Sleeping Under the Tree of Life*, ed. L. Timmel Duchamp, Aqueduct Press, 2016.

“And Not Fear the Night” was the keynote speech for the Memphis Juneteenth Afrofuturism Gala 2022 in Memphis, TN, a version of which was shared at the 2022 Guest of Honor and Awards Dessert Salon at WisCon 45 in Madison, WI.

“The Dragon Can't Dance” first appeared in *Transition: The Magazine of Africa and the Diaspora*, no. 115, Hutchins Center, Harvard University, 2015.

“Child's Play” first appeared in *Eleven Eleven: A Journal of Literature and Art*, no. 12, ed. Hugh Behm-Steinberg, California College of the Arts, 2012. It was reprinted in Sheree Renée Thomas, *Nine Bar Blues: Stories from an Ancient Future*, Third Man Books, 2020.

“Thirteen Year Long Song” first appeared in Thomas, *Nine Bar Blues.*

“River, Clap Your Hands” first appeared in *Stories for Chip: A Tribute to Samuel R. Delany*, ed. Nisi Shawl and Bill Campbell, Rosarium Publishing, 2015, and was reprinted in Sheree Renée Thomas, *Sleeping Under the Tree of Life*, Aqueduct Press, 2016.

“Forrest” first appeared in “*Roots + Resistance” issue, About Place Journal* 5, no. 2, ed. Lauren Camp and Melissa Tuckey, Black Earth Institute, 2018.

All others appear for the first time in this collection.

The Tongue I Dream In

ISBN (paperback): 979-8-88744-195-5
ISBN (e-book): 979-8-88744-209-9
LCCN: 2026934328

Series editors: Nisi Shawl and Nick Mamatas
Cover design by John Yates/www.stealworks.com
Author photo by Danian Darrell Jerry
Insides by Jonathan Rowland

10 9 8 7 6 5 4 3 2 1

Printed in the USA

CONTENTS

To Jacqueline, for the gift of the first tongue.

To Jackie B. and Jada, for the fire and the future. You are the blood's deep melody, the rhythm of my waking, and the reason I have a story worth telling.

The Tongue We Dream In

Our first language was wet
mournful questions rang
like falling stars
in red clay throats

No milk teeth to help
form words, our eyes
made syllables, cries strung out
on ropes of tears, thoughts
dangled on twisted threads
of hope

Our first language was touch
balled fists of unlined fingers
grasping for fire, tendrils of light
blazed in eyes, molten with liquid fear
skin pricked and pierced with
stories to be told, lives to unfold
through the dark tunnel of years

Our first language was song
a bell hangs in our hearts
rings with every bloody drumbeat

songs to reduce souls to ashes
and songs to sing them anew

Our first language
was wet touch singing
ourselves across the darkness
into life, in our dreams we sing
in the first tongue, the language
before birth

And Not Fear the Night*

LISTEN,

The river is a witness.

Let me tell you a story, a *jigjack waterback* tale of a people who walked on water, across the Big Wata, back to their homeland they called Guinee. Let me tell you of a mighty, muddy river where a Black river goddess sings each night day, bringing the news of her daughters 'round the world, calling weary spirits, the restless and the wanderlusters on home, to travel beyond. Let me tell you of the people who could fly, those who ate the magic okra seed and blossomed until they climbed trees that sang and danced. Black-eyed peas and spirit seeds, those who could see ancient stars from far away long before telescopes were designed to perceive them.

Let me tell you about North Memphis, community of my birth, of haints who sit on your chest at 3:33 a.m. and stare deep into your eyes, daring you to blink, to breathe, to speak, to move, whispering secrets and magic that your family has tried to keep hidden for generations.

Let me tell you about alien sisters journeying on an eternal quest through the stars, seeking the most magical music of all, let me tell you of immortal DJs, ancient instruments, midnight deals at the crossroads, let me tell you about Robert Johnson's three

* Juneteenth Afrofuturism Gala, Tone / BSAM (Beale Street Landing, Mississippi River) keynote speech, 2022.

graves, a ravenous melusine, and a muse so cold, so fine, you don't mind that she exacts a most curious price.

Listen,

Somewhere there is a star child gazing in the sky

Searching for songs that might teach them how to fly
Somehow, teach the star child to sing and not fear the night

Not fear the night, not fear the night
as we are gathered here tonight across the river.
Look and listen, to your left, to your right.
See and feel the warmth of those smiling faces,
their hope and the vision they contain

We are still here. We have survived.

Friends, may we build for a more prosperous, healthy, equitable, beautiful future, may we thrive!

Let us gather together and tell the stories that lift and sing, tell the stories that heal and mend, the broken parts of all of us. Let us work to tell the stories that help us remember the lost and found parts of the community. Let us rise when we fall. Let us hold each other accountable, naming and claiming the hurt but also naming and claiming the healing.

Let us not fear the night. Because the night is just another side of the sun.

And while we are not promised tomorrow, the future awaits, infinite in the fresh seeds we plant today. Walk in that faith. Let us create the art and the stories that sing and dance, the music that lives inside each one of you, carry you on into the stars of possibility.

Possibility.

If you are a fellow Memphian, then your story is like my story. We come from a spiritual people, of those who had no choice but to make the possible out of the impossible, a people of deep faith and a lot of dark humor. We had to laugh to keep from crying. *Let me say that again*, we had to laugh to keep from crying. We wore the mask, but that mask is slipping. With the past few years we have witnessed, I know you can appreciate what that means.

We are born and live in a city whose public face has always been us—our culture, our music, our story, our songs, our dance and rhythms, the hymns and hums ringing and shouting out and up through our tears, our labor, our vision, our blood.

And yet, we don't own most of these public-facing buildings, these museums and cultural institutions that hold our history, that speak on the experiences that created those bloodsongs through the ages. We are the face, we wear the mask, and the cycle repeats and repeats. But here, among these giving, growing, gifted hands, we build upon old traditions of our elders, we take their wisdom and we add more agency, more audacity, more ambition, and brick-by-brick we are adding a new floor to the foundation they have passed on to us across the generations. We are in the heart of our community, building straight for the stars. I ask . . .

What are the stories you told yourself to keep going, to not remain paralyzed in anger, in power-less-ness, and in fear?

To not fear the night?

What are those star-rimmed stories of tomorrows not yet seen?

We laugh to keep from crying. We create art to fight erasure. We create art to fight the silences that kill. We fight to create art that makes visible the invisible, that places the margins in the center, the art that answers the questions of those asking years. Thank you, Zora! Thank you Ida B! Thank you, Memphis!

This is how we survived the traumas and a nightmarish history in this world. This is how we wrote new stories to counter the ones that smiled and laughed as they tried to kill dignity, humanity, justice, us.

There was always light, always joy. Sometimes expressed in the church and sometimes expressed elsewhere, in the backwoods, under the moonlight in a circle of trees, at the ring shout, voices flung up to the stars, stepping counterclockwise, mighty rootwork spinning this world round with our voices, with our will to survive, to thrive, to bravely speak the plain truth, to create space that *creates space*, that holds us and upholds us. This art, this living.

There's a sense of greater things, definitely more powerful than we as a species may ever truly understand, but the mystery won't stop us from trying to do so. It's that mystery and magic, that weirdness that makes me curious, and it's something I lean into and explore when it feels right, in my writing on and off the page, and in my editorial work: communal service that is not about gatekeeping but work that is about crashing the gates open, flinging the doors wide so brilliance and imagination and audacity can *shimmy-shimmy be-bop* on through.

My vision, my art, my intention comes in part from my ancestors, who have shown me at the most challenging of times how much they believe in and love me. I know that I walk in this world not alone. There are good people, brilliant people like Victoria Jones and all of the brilliant hands and minds that help make TONE, the Memphis and global BSAM Black Speculative Arts community, the Kheprw Institute, Afrofuturism 2.0 and all the 0's to come. I'm not their wildest dream, shit, they dreamed of freedom! But I am grateful for all our ancestors, for all my dear grandparents, my mother and my father, my aunts and uncles, my siblings and favorite cousins, the Backsliders and Scripture-quoters, the Let-it-be-what-it's-gon'-be folks, the Leave-that-child-alone folks who helped remind me that all of those unheralded ways of seeing and being are important in recreating and reimagining the world on and off the page. Worlds of fantasy that feel like truth. And that creator spark is nurtured and inspired in childhood, so let us keep our children's dream spaces safe, fertile ground for the future.

There's something powerful and a little frightening in all of it, in this storytelling, in creation, no matter the form, the medium, the genre. In the old haints and too-horrible-but-its-true tales that my grandfather and his friends, neighbors would share back in North Memphis, in the city where I was born, the city that killed King. As a child coming of age in the '70s, I had to learn how to reconcile the all-too-real horrors of the city with the entertainment we enjoyed on the TV screen. I think it's no coincidence that the Black horror films and series we are seeing today each explore how the very act of us existing is often the source of the horror. Blackness in these films and series is the catalyst, Black progress and Black excellence are the motivating forces and that's been true in real life in more ways than we like to tell. For us, reality is the real scary stuff. The real monsters are not hiding beneath our beds, sometimes they walk among us, and they try to terrorize from within, planting fear in your own head.

But there is also joy! Embracing what makes us whole again, what makes us feel real in a realm of phantoms, is what brings that light. I remain grateful for the writers who remind us to have hope and wonder in these darkening days. Beacons in the journey included Zora and Walker, Morrison and Jones, Dumas, Reed, Baraka and Bradbury, Butler and Delany, Clifton, Marquez, and Rushdie, Hopkinson, Hairston, Flowers, and so many voices whose writing transported me, sparked my imagination, and led me to the work that has been described as speculative fiction, Afrofuturism, Africanfuturism.

Afrofuturists reimagine old gods and journey beyond colonial borders, space, and time. They choreograph new movements and reexamine traditional narratives, excavating the past to observe the rhythms of our present. With an eye toward the future and an ear for the songs and lessons of the past, these future-focused artists from around the world create a sense of wonder and curiosity, recasting the challenges of today with new mythologies and technology, offering readers exciting new heroes to explore as they embark upon thrilling, unknown adventures.

Lately, I have been asked to speak on the power and the role of Afrofuturism. As if to say, what can Afrofuturism do for us in the face of all of this—a reality we, gathered here in Memphis, know intimately: the political machinations, the encroaching fascism, the pervasive racism, and the intentional assaults on the health and wealth of Black families and communities across the nation and around the world, from despots whose culture thrives on zero-sum games, exploitation, and scarcity—not on community progress, excellence, and abundance. Those triggered by Black prosperity and success, sabotaging every milestone we reach, every success we make, all while pretending that failure is our inescapable legacy.

May I suggest that this body of creative work, this lens with which to view the world can serve as our memory and as foresight, forging the way for new, creative pathways into the futures we hope to be.

As we gather here, we must act with intention. We must work to rekindle hope in the wake of terror. We who are bewildered and heartbroken must remain determined in the face of unchecked violence and its circular nature.

How does art lift and protect us, inform and inspire us? How does art create space in the midst of a public health crisis, historically institutionalized racism, and a legion of phobias that bind and kill, and the insidious public policies designed to criminalize Black history and culture, defund and dismantle programs for Black citizens, and erase our very presence from public space—attacks on civil rights that extend to the core amendments of the Constitution itself, even manifesting in mass deportations designed to fragment and diminish our nation's living ties to the global diaspora?

Afrofuturism, its art and its vision, around the world, gave me hope during the tumultuous early years of the COVID pandemic and in the wake of the social unrest following the deaths of George Floyd, Breonna Taylor, Elise Malary, Tatiana LaBelle, Tyre Nichols, and others. This work is remembrance and resurrection, resistance and restored hope, imagination versus nihilism, in a social, economic, and political landscape of uprisings and upheaval, strange fruit buried in scorched earth.

The artists and writers who create this original work ask the essential questions that plague us all. What ancient and familiar new blossoms will spring up from the change the world demands now? What sacrifices and compromises will be made in the days ahead? Our work is a clarion call for dignity, equality, and justice. It is a cry for rest, self-care, and balance. It is a celebration of our journey, past, present, and future, and it speaks to the temporal and systemic changes that must come to pass throughout the diaspora in order to birth futures where Black lives truly matter.

Some of the most inspiring work I have read was written by brilliant writers who I have come to think of as dangerous muses. Dangerous because they challenge the stories our nation tells itself and that the rest of our world consumes whether its wants to or not. They flip the script by choosing when and where they will enter, writing works in which they are the universal stories, where they are subjects of their own epic tales.

Black women writers, innovators in the field of world-breaking and world-making, are creating some of the best, most memorable twenty-first-century speculative fiction of the day. Beyond the theoretical and the abstract, this Afrofuturism is rooted in Black bodies, Black experiences, Black identities. Their work is exhilarating and imaginative, well-crafted and conceived, and often beautifully, beautifully written.

These writers have captured the human spirit on the page, while delving into Afrodiasporic ancestral roots. Their stories and novels are written in the tradition of Black feminism and womanism, and they continue to expand our understanding of Afrofuturism and what this exciting body of work can be. *What is possible.* These Black women writers, dangerous muses all, write stories set among the stars peopled by women and communities we not only know intimately, but love.

If you leave with nothing else tonight, please leave with the intention to read more work by dangerous muses. I believe your life will be enriched in this exciting exploration.

In my own research journeys, I learned that the Indigenous people from the Chippewa to the Dogon have shared epic stories of star people birthed from afar. Believing that their pharaohs became stars in the Northern sky after death, ancient Egyptians aligned their temples and pyramids due north toward the "indestructible" pole stars. After a lifelong fascination with science fiction, deep historical excavation, and reverse engineering of recorded memory through the lens of the imagination, I think our genre has the power to offer us a greater understanding not only of our world, but of ourselves.

A mind or a soul is a changing prism; it becomes more itself over time. Speculative fiction reminds us that we are part of a greater world beyond the one beneath our feet. And with nearly every element in the human body made from stars, many coming from several supernovas, this sentiment is more fact than fiction. For ultimately, each of us is that star child gazing at the sky, dreaming of that place from whence we all come.

Listen,

Deep inside, can you *hear*, can you *feel* it? Deep within there is a tightening, a release from gravity's pull. That is letting go of the things that hold us from the work and the stories that force us to reach and climb.

Now look, up and out there, can you see it? No? Well, imagine it! That is the light from whence we came and the light to which we will return. May our journeys around the star we call the sun continue to enlighten and inspire us in this work we do, and may it keep us encouraged, brave enough to carry on, never fearing *the night.*

Thank you!

Gorgon Root

Was it the way light caught
in the deep-river bend of her hair
each helix a history spun tight
a midnight garden blooming defiance
before serpent-song filled the air?
They whispered histories must be tamed
a shroud for the sun-fed constellation
lest its gravity pull empires down.

Or did the goddess envy the hum
the low thrumming beneath the scalp
a power rooted deeper than reverence?
The curse arrived like frost on glass
blurring the view until admiration
soured into something sharp-fanged
misreading abundance as attack
beauty refracted into threat.

Now the gaze that greets her calcifies.
It is not Perseus' shield flashing bright
but the blue-white glare striping the tarmac
the sterile hum of fluorescent tubes overhead
leaching the color from her skin

breath held captive in the throat's narrow passage
a slow turning inward to stone.

She walks through rooms where the air thins
pressed flat between the pages of old tales
a silhouette sketched by fear not fact.
The weight of it a phantom limb
aching where vibrant parts were judged
condemned exiled before a word was spoken
the echo of judgment a cold draft.

This geography they demand be paved smooth
flattened into acquiescence, assimilation
this map of kinship intricate and wild.
Deny the kink the curl the coil
the living testament that refuses erasure
that defies gravity, growing upward
reaching for the sun.
But the roots run deep beneath the surface
drawing water from unseen wells.

Medusa knows the mirror's cruel trick
how it captures the watcher's own fear.
Banished she seeks not a cave but breathable air
a sky wide enough to hold her whole undisguised self
while the world still sharpens its swords
mistaking her heartbeat for thunder.

Receipts for Stolen Sunlight

I remember shadows stitched to sunlight mandates whispered
To bind the coils eclipse the glory tame the brightness down
Lest beauty worn too easy stir the envious gods
Or incite a power rooted wilder than their laws could reach
My own shimmer judged too potent even then
A threat needing the shroud the curse the serpent's hiss
Before they learned to covet what they first condemned.

That old dissecting gaze still lands sharp—mirrored now
In cold blue rivers scrolling, feeding, hungry eyes.
No longer just the town square, or the master's assessing glance
But myriad screens that pin down, sample, steal the light
Cataloging living art, filing its soul away.
My own reflection fractured, sold in market stalls
While these bright daughters walk beaded galaxies ablaze.

They called this magic common loud a garish thing
Remember whispers snickers turning backs on streets
This vibrant pulse deemed noise this rhythm born of joy
The swing of gold geometry against the throat
The patient maps woven strand by living strand
Now see it lifted soulless rinsed of context sweat and tears
Worn empty hollowed out by ghosts afraid of fire.

How long must living beauty see itself returned?
As pale cold copies crowned with celebrated names
A curated theft that drains the color, claims the husk.
This tired cycle turning admiration into ash . . .
My own head brandished: trophy, weapon, talisman.
My essence warped to serve the very gaze I'd freeze.
I watch my daughters now and taste the ancient rage
And ask the weary question for them: When?

When does this hunger cease that craves the fruit, denies the root?
This echo chamber trading bitter envy for applause.
I watch her walk, resilience braided in her hair
A living archive turning toward the hostile sun.
She carries centuries, breathes defiance, meets their stares.
My gaze sharpens with hers, assessing hollow claims
And holds the weight of stone remembering its power:
To fix the truth, expose the lie, defend its own.

A Strange Brutal Grace

I.

We move through this Ship's belly, this long metallic
gasp between worlds, breathing manufactured air thick
with the static cling of history's chains, ghosts reforged
as hull integrity, pressure seals measured precisely.
They call it progress, this steady regulated orbit
circling Mars' red indifferent face, this digital tether
tight around the soul's slow spiral toward forgetting.
But the skin remembers, don't it?
Holds the raised scar the memory burn, the lash under starlight
filtered weak, diffused through engineered domes
designed to mimic a home never known.
A strange grace, this is, survival counted in rationed cycles
in patched-up life support humming low constant dirges.

This Ship breathes metal sighs a long lung collapsing slow
between indifferent stars we float, suspended animation
orbiting Mars red eye glaring back, no welcome mat
just rust dust silence measured in parsecs light years lost
from shores we only know through brittle data ghosts
grandmama's songs humming low beneath the engine drone
They say forget Earth forget the Sun lazy man's head

thrown high forget Moon, the Returner, forget sky
as solid blue rock dome pierced with breathing holes
for spirit light

Here sky is viewport readouts, radiation warnings
hull integrity, Stars mere fusion
distant cold equations plotted clean
not !Kung porcupines alive with spines
not ant lions watching hungry
not ancestors walking the bright ash path
flung across the night
That old lore outlawed now forbidden code
dangerous memory like our skin, our hair
our unsanctioned rhythms rising anyway

II.

A brutal grace, too often turned inward, blade-sharp
like found metal honed rough back on Earth.
We forget Ship bleeds oxygen from all of us
Below, Topshelf, same indifferent engine
grinding spirit down to data points.
We learn to fashion curses from our deepest wellspring of pain
target the brother, sister, cousin, child who shares this recycled air
this close-quartered funk, this memory-ache, this future endlessly deferred.
Yes, we know this wound intimately, this turning on the self, oldest trick
the overseer taught, transplanted light years off course
flung far from that first violated soil.

But another grace persists, stubborn weed in hydroponic tube
It finds the conjure in the flickering console light remembers
blessing oil for hands cracked dry like Delta earth

makes altar bright with scavenged wire plastic hope shards gleaned
It braids the children's hair tight against the low-g pull
whispers true names, defiant sound against
the static wash, the mandated forgetting

It finds the Lion's Eyes Mura burning fierce in Scorpius' tail
reads futures in the dust motes dancing slow in weak lumen light
It beats the deck plate floor with ghost drum rhythm calls down rain
imagines flight on wings not made of metal but of story bone deep knowing
This grace insists remembers, reclaims, remakes the world inside a universe
held tight behind the eyes, fierce and enduring, strange, yes, brutal often
but ours alone, our navigation chart, our breathing room, our saving.

And the grace yet strange forged in that first fire
crossing water honed brutal on the auction block
the breaking field, the project stairwell translated
now to Ship's thin recycled air, this vertical drift
It cuts sometimes, turns inward, sharpest edge first
we measure wounds, compare the depth of loss
whose Maafa hurts most, speak the colonizer's math of lack
prosecutor judge jury in these cramped corridors passing sentence
on our own blood kin, forgetting Ship drains all life feeds
the Core Below starves the Topshelf thin
This reflex deep, this inherited poison
a brutal grace that lets us stand at all after the breaking

III.

Remember sky wasn't always cold
calculated equation, vacuum threat?
Grandmama whispered stars were pinpricks
breathing holes punched in the solid blue rock ceiling
resting gently on the world's edge.
The Nyae Nyae knew, the /Xam saw stars as tiny
bright-spined creatures, as ant lions hunting
falling to Earth each morning as insects.
Sky held families then, stories, warnings
not just cold fusion reactions, empty parsecs
trajectories plotted neat.

This Ship's view-slit shows only hungry infinity
maybe the rings like cosmic scar tissue, beautiful
terrible, circling Saturn, that gas giant's slow, unwitnessing spin.
We try sometimes to read them still
for omens, augury's forgotten grammar
but the language of Ship's command, programmed long ago
left little room for spirit work, no bandwidth allocated for stars
that watch you back, that know your name.

Still, the body keeps its own defiant cosmology.
The heart beats out old stubborn rhythms
drum talk deep beneath the hum.
We find the conjure in the circuit board's
unpredictable spark, braid forgotten meaning back
into the children's coiled hair, whisper true names
soft against the broadcast orders demanding silence
assimilation, forgetting.

Plant seeds saved from memory's dwindling packet
in nutrient paste, pray for impossible bloom
against the odds, in this fabricated air.
It ain't gentle, ain't neat, this necessary flowering
in the long dark transit between promised
perhaps phantom, lands.
It is the grace of jagged edges, hard-learned resistance
yes, a brutal beauty ground sharp enough maybe
to cut clean through the static, carve a new frequency
make us finally seen, fiercely whole, vibrantly alive
right here, orbiting now.

Jigganaut

"Because my feet are gay with dancing, you do not know I die?"
—Langston Hughes, "The Dream Keeper"

When Mama say, *I dance.*

I press my toe in Uncle Bo Bo's shoe and jump and bow, the ole jim crow. When Mama say reel, *I reel.* I leap and squat, turn and stop, flap my arms way up like a chicken, dancing to the beat. Mama take the black soot and rub it all over my face. Mama take the black soot and smear it cross my chin. It feel cold at first, cold like the air outside our window, then it warm up when I sweat. Mama say I can fan my hands and wave and wave at the people laughing, but I can't wipe my face, can't scratch my face, no matter how much the black soot itch. Mama don't want nobody to see the black of my skin. She say, the black God give us ain't good enough. She say, the folk outside don't want to see *real black*, they want to see ole black, *ole joe black.*

I don't know who Joe is, but he sho'll is black! I never seen nobody black as this. The black outside Ship ain't even black as this. Never seen it, but Mama have. She say, when she was real little, when she was maybe even littler than me, Mama say she saw *real black* long time ago, so long, she said folk didn't even live inside. They lived outside, out in the night. She say sometime, when they stand out there, a star made them blacker. She said folk used to stand outside all day and just get blacker and blacker and it didn't hurt and nobody even cared at all. Wayback when. *Black was beautiful.*

"Come on, Nene."

That Mama. She poke her head in the dressing room and stare at my face. She squinting like that star shining in her eye, like it too bright to see. I think I look the same, but I ain't sure. Maybe I'm not black enough? If it's not black, *ole joe black*, the folk don't laugh. If I don't jump and bow, reel real fast enough, the folk don't even smile. They just look and stare, look like the star in their eye, like that old star shine so bright, the light fill the sky full of tears.

But sometimes, when Mama think about them Wayback days, and she get that shine-eye look, that quivery-eye and poke-lip look, then the tears start falling, and she cry. Hate to see my mama cry. She hate it too, cuz when that happens, dancing is hard. Hard-hard work. Cuz then the ole joe black drips some, and the stains get all over our suits. Then Mama have to find a big fake flower or some kind of ribbon to stick on there and cover up. But you can't cover up heartache and you can't cover black tears . . . *O, Mary, don't you weep* cuz then Mama forget her lines and she can't hardly sing no songs, and then we don't get no tips. *Because her mouth wide with laughter, her throat full of pain.* All that practicing and rehearsing just to wind up with weak applause and no credits.

You can't survive on Ship with just the clapping of hands. Yo dancing gots to *move.*

Director say we can't make white folks feel bad. If they feelings get hurt just one little bitty bit, it's *curtains*. And curtains ain't good. Curtains mean we don't eat none of that good Topshelfer food in the club, and we have to go all the way back down to our old sector on the Ship, down in the bows, levels below, closer to the Ship's center—hungrier than before we first came.

So we Juba dis and Juba dat and wear the mask of black stars. Cake-walking Topshelf ain't easy. Mama say we gots to be more than a minstrel man. So we sing and dance and tap and jump and reel, spinning across the stage almost as fast as Ship spinning through space. They say we going somewhere, but getting there is the mystery—ain't no telling when. Mama say I might live long enough to see where that is, but she don't expect to. Say sometimes when we spinning, if you in the right place—and the right place *always with the Topshelfers*—then you can see the mystery planet up on the Observation Decks. Mama say it's a red place they call Mars. Red like the lipstick Director and the audience like us to wear. Red smiles on our black faces and wide, wide eyes.

When we dance, we got to pretend like we don't see—*them* laughing and pointing at us. When I was little, it used to make me cry. I don't cry no more. *Because my mouth wide with laughter, my throat deep with song.*

"Maybe you gon' see it one day," Mama say, "the place they all going to, and if you do, sang a song and do a new dance for me."

It worries me when she talk like that. I don't want to be nowhere without Mama, sho'll nuff not alone on this Ship. Ain't hardly no children to play with. Don't seem like there's that many of us left here. At least not on our level. Ship is big though, ain't no telling who all here. Mama say we must dance to remind the audience of the times when there were more of us, the times when black folks did more than just jump jim crow and reel and dance.

Mama say there used to be whole cities of black folk, nations, and islands, too. With names and songs that only our folks know, secret names that say one thing but mean another. Mama say a lot of things, secrets I don't always understand. She say I'm too little now but I won't always be. She say the Knowing come when the Spirit moves you, when your insides move just as smooth as your outside can.

Sometimes I dream of those Wayback folks. I wonder how somebody can get so mad, they change the laws to make a whole group of people just go away. *Poof, whoosh, begone!* Mama say first they was happy. With no more black folks, they thought all their problems was solved. No more black faces to remind them of who they used to be, and all the time in the world to discover who they really was. But then . . . not much was solved, cuz people still gon' be just people, and Mama say they started to miss us.

"Miss black folks?" I say. "What they miss?" And Mama just wave her hand as if everybody and nobody know. She start doing the ucklebuck and the buzzard lope, bent over, arms flapping low and wild, make me laugh and laugh until I join her.

"Strange ain't it, how you don't miss yo water 'til your well run dry." Mama say them folks came in all shades of black and sang songs in many different languages and danced like their insides could move as smooth as their outside do. *Spirit dance!* Danced so good, everybody wanted to copy. Thousands she say. Millions. Back then, all kinds of folks wanted to be black, too. Everybody want to be black, don't nobody want to be black. They want everything but the burden. But that's the part that mess me up. If they love us, why they hate us, why they make us go away?

If I lived in Wayback, I'd visit all the lands and learn every tongue, every language, and do every single dance. Now there's just a few of us, and look all we do is dance.

Mama say first they took our rights (I'm not so sure what that is, and Mama get quivery, shivery star-eyed every time she 'bout to say). Then they took our property, our homes (she said we didn't all used to live on Ship) and our businesses and jobs (when *we* was Director and *we* decided how we'd spend our nights and days) and all the things in between. Including our names. We was dee-lee-gimmy-mut. Can't nothing black exist no mo. The end of blackness was a big hit. So big, they had to bring it back so they could wipe it away again.

Mama and me do a secret number on it—but I can't never tell Director or it be *curtains*, and me and Mama will never jump the jim crow or dance ever again. It's a special kind of shuffle, the kind of dance that make me feel like I'm doing backflips on the inside, all in my heart and my mind. And when we do that dance, we only do it with Sun House, the One Arm Dancing Sensation. He one of the best dancers up here. It's all heel-toe-*shuffle-shuffle*-jazz hands-and-*smiles.* 'Cept you float, float, showboating in the air, like yo feets got wings and your whole body pulled by invisible god strings. All the patrons from Ship pile in and grab their tables to see Mama, Sun House, and me dance. Regulars way up front so they can see everything and hear the music real good. Sometimes I close my eyes real tight, and then it feel like I'm gon' float on up and touch the sky.

If our bandleader Tubbs and n'em can't play no more, Director pumps in not-so-live music in the loudspeakers and it's blast off, *lights camera act shun* time. No matter the music, we got to dance anyway. Mama call this routine another one our secret Hid Way Up All In They Face dances. The song played is my favorite cuz Mama helped Tubbs write it. It make my insides feel almost good as my outside do. Mama named it after a Wayback bluesman, a poet who lived in a tall man's town. Mama say poems ain't nothing but the heart's song with no music, says sometimes yo own voice the only sound and that's just fine, "Cuz your voice is an instrument, Nene, and when you ready, it's a weapon."

I don't know what that means yet, but when I do . . . *wooo weee*! I'ma dance up a storm in this Ship.

Mama remember poems from Wayback. She make her own tunes with them. She tells Tubbs and he arranges them all nice so we can keep the show fresh. Director likes that. Sometimes he gives us extra credits when the audience really whoops and hollers. That's when we be showing out. Like our Hid Way Up In Yo Face dance, the reel Mama called, "You Done Took Our Blues & Gone." She loves this dance, and I love it, too, cuz anytime we get those shimmy-shimmy star-eyes, or when the laughter gets too loud and ain't no love or no joy in it, we just shuffle along and do our dance, we jump and reel jim crow, smiling with our bright red lips, holding a secret that only God knows.

The Dragon Can't Dance

THE FIRST TIME I danced, I hated it. Six years old, skinny as a string bean, shy, observant, the last thing I wanted was to be pulled into my nana's long, strong arms and swept onto the makeshift dance floor at her birthday party. My hair was tightly braided, laced with the new gold and white beads Mama bought just for the occasion. My freshly oiled temples smelled like heaven, hurt like hell. Coconut and mango braids throbbed with the beat that thumped from wood veneer speakers sprawled across two wobbly card tables in a corner of the garden. Nana threw back her head and pranced, that's right, pranced past my two uncles, my sisters, Papa and Mama, past all her old neighbors and church friends, and rolled her ample hips like a much younger woman. I was scandalized! Everyone clap clapped and howled at the vision, bellies full of roti and spicy jerk chicken. Nana wore red. And she looked amazing, a juicy hibiscus blossom in her hair.

"Four score! Four score!" she cried, channeling Lincoln or the Bible. The sparkly eight and zero bobbed and weaved on her rainbow crown. In her birthday hat, she looked like a goddess or a ten-year-old, I could not tell which, before she reached for me, and I was swept into the swirl of sweat and laughter, the deep pulsing music, the mass of warm brown arms and legs, fiercely dancing in her herb garden behind her brownstone in Brooklyn. As she tugged and jerked my freshly cocoa-buttered arms back and forth, a wicked puppeteer, I was mortified. Not like the time I spilled soda on my white skirt at school, and the big girls pointed and teased me, shouting "Sanaa started her period! Sanaa started her peer-ree-odd!" It seemed as if everyone in Crown Heights had gathered to see my humiliation. They say the dragon can't dance. At six, neither could I.

But that was then.

#

Thinking about it now, I cannot believe how much love I took for granted. I'm talking about real love, the kind you can touch with your own hands and feel its arms around you and breathe in. When Nana made me dance at her eightieth birthday party, I was so embarrassed, so afraid I'd make a fool of myself, that her joyful, public love of me felt more like a slap than a celebration. While other kids tap-danced and moonwalked over the old *children should be seen and not heard* thing, bucked and clamored for adult attention, *any* attention, I preferred back then to recede into darkness, to be the silent night that cloaked the bright lone star. Nana wasn't having none of that. When she pulled me into her arms that smelled like cinnamon, sweet milk and lime, I was angry. I felt exposed, naked.

Dancing exposes you. In dancing, your body, traitor flesh that it is, reveals all the things your spirit tries to hide. Drawn from the margins into the center of my big family's love and laughter, all the vulnerabilities, all the hopes and questions, all the fire spark of early, tentative temptations flowed through me, flowed out of me—and I hated it.

Then.

Then the drumbeats in my feet, the longing to fly that flamed through my limbs, possessed me. The sensation singed skin, engulfed my anxiety, burnt away my invisible cloak. After that night, dancing became addictive.

#

Me and my girls, we used to turn up, shut it down right there in Goat Park. While the boys were out on the asphalt, sweating and cursing, checking bricks and trying to dunk in their throwback Jordans, we would be over by the raggedy ass slide, far away from crying babies and fussing nannies cussing in their mother tongues, but close enough for the fine boys to see us, making moves, moving in time, and imitating our favorites. Chanel could fract better than anybody. Her arms and hands flying in precise, quickfast patterns. Her sharp elbows were arrows that pierced the air; even her long spiraling locs swung in time to her rhythm. Bijou's neck and thighs were like that old-school silly putty. She could stretch and slide, whine and grind like she was all water, not bones and flesh. Me, I was the choreographer, always been, always will be. Sanaa, Queen of the Stans. I could do all my girls' moves and then some I never shared. Even back then, I dreamed new steps and stans in my sleep, woke up counting beats and wrecking rhythms, even when I brushed my teeth.

To dance was to live.

Other younger girls and little children sometimes watched us from the sidelines, tried to mimic our moves. None of them had enough booty yet, the extra bounce for the ounce that added that special polyrhythm. But I wasn't stingy. I taught anyone who wanted to learn and have fun, and some of them were really very good.

Back then, I gave my moves away for free.

"Might as well," Bijou used to say. "They gon' steal it anyway."

Chanel disapproved, flinging her locs back to underline the point. "You can't give away everything, Sanaa. Some stuff you got to keep for yourself."

It was when they asked us to perform at the Rucker Park Streetball Fest, an annual fundraiser against police brutality, for the families of the latest victims, that it all changed. That's when Isis first saw me. We couldn't believe that Ice came to Manigault. Her appearance was completely unannounced; otherwise she and the Goat would have been swamped by fans and paparazzi. She was promoting her upcoming release and would be the celebrity judge for the tournament. Everyone and their mama, folk who know damn well they couldn't ball or stan, was trying to get up in that competition. It was chaos. Harlem was out of control. There was no way they were going to be able to hold the people back, but we weren't ordinary people. I had been waiting for a chance like this since beyond forever, and now here it was. I had no idea just how long it would go on being that way.

#

While the seconds counted down before curtains, my stomach filled with a hundred steely butterflies. Their wings shredded my confidence, then my doubts. After collaborating with Isis for so long, I still felt anxious, still felt the nervousness before I was tasked to move the crowd—her crowd. But just like the times when I battled street crews with Chanel in Goat Park on the West Side and with Bijou on the drummer's hill in Harlem, my nervousness was quickly replaced with extreme focus. When green zeros filled the air above me, I watched our splendid bodies explode into action. As I moved, I almost forgot that the force behind Isis's explosion was my own.

Under my stage lights, my skin glistened like blue-black diamonds. I did the counts in my head, allowing Isis's music to flow through me, flow with me. Inside my crystal cave—a geodesic chamber lined with adaptive optical arrays that served as both immersive display and multispectrum sensor—as I called the room designed for my unseen solo performances, I danced with only the barest of clothing. Dark brown threads designed to wick sweat, designed to match my skin, monitored and transmitted my every movement via embedded micro-conductors woven into the very fabric. These biometric garments pulsed faintly, mapping muscle contractions and nerve impulses to Isis without hindering my movement. I was the behind-the-scenes choreographer and the spotlit superstar—all at once. As a child, like many girls, I used to dance in the middle of my room, until one of my sisters would walk in. Then I would stop for a moment and giggle, then begin the dance again as if no one was there. As I danced alone, I was the brightest star, the only star in my imagination. In the crystal cave, whose walls sparkled with light and data streaming from the optical arrays and pulsed with the music's rhythm, the illusion was the same. In the cave, I was the puppet and the puppeteer, a tamed dragon.

Instead of breathing fire, I was the flame.

Management wanted to install climate control, to reduce the possibility of my sweat damaging the software and equipment—specifically the sensitive floor sensors and the delicate fiber connections linking my suit to the primary transmitter. Under our special contract, "unprecedented" my agent had said, there was a severe gag order—proprietary tech (whispers of bio-kinematic translation and neural network mirroring) and cloak-and-dagger secrecy—and clause after clause after clause. So many fine points and legalese that I finally signed it when my agent emphasized the unprecedented number of zeros that would grace my first check.

Management was worried about me damaging the equipment, but no one was worried about the equipment damaging me. Climate control for their suit. Ksst! I laughed at this, said I preferred to sweat. Authentic biosignatures probably enhanced the data stream, gave it that edge. Surely they had insurance for cosmic funk. They pushed back. I pushed harder then. It would make the dance more authentic, and Isis, despite her meteoric rise, needed all the help she could get. My dance was born in New York's streets, channeled fractals from across the nation, adopted traditions from around the world, reimagined Ailey and Dunham, Jamison and Jackson reborn as starship troopers, flinging their black bodies through space. Isis was born in the city of a thousand suns, her voice quickly becoming the anthem of a legion. To deliver, I needed to feel the salt water beading on my skin, to feel the fire coursing through me.

I needed it far more than Isis and her backup dancers, gifted girls who twirled and stamped in perfect synchronized steps derived from my core movements but filtered through predictive algorithms. I watched as the dancers performed my choreography, as Isis, the blazing star, performed my steps mere nanoseconds after my own movements, the delay an unavoidable consequence of signal travel time and atmospheric processing, the ocean between us.

Mistress of my crystal cave with its vital signs monitors and cords, its floor-to-ceiling screens reflecting the sold-out concert stage and the audience that screamed four thousand miles away in Freetown, I could see the stadium reflected all around me. Each set for Isis was a variation of an ancient Egyptian or other pseudo-African theme. Over the last of our forty city tour, the world had seen Nubians and Pharaonic Pyramids, Dogon masks and references to alien close encounters with the inhabitants of the Dog Star, Sirius.

The last show in Paris had Isis lounging on Napoleon's tomb, surrounded by obelisks and giant replicas of herself. Tonight's show in Sierra Leone, diamond capital of the world for centuries, was an ahistorical remix of surrounding nations. Our biggest number—my biggest number—would find Isis rising up from a rolling pink lake like the one in Senegal, its waves carrying her up to the base of a skyscraper-sized baobab tree that held her throne. *All praise Isis, Queen of Life.* For her finale she would appear to break into a hundred pieces, then resurrect herself for the last song.

Even though Isis could not create her own dance, I knew better than anyone how good she was at creating her own myth. Friendships, family, and fans, she hustled them as deftly as a goddess. All were ripe for sacrifice.

"We sisters," she had said when I had mustered courage enough to tell her I was gone. Even her voice had taken on my cadence. She could code-switch with the best. "You need me, I need you. Sanaa, Na-Na, they can't do this without us. I can't do this without you."

I guess Management had told her I was serious this time, so Isis made a special live-in-the-flesh personal visit to me. It had been a long time. It caught me by surprise, and I was angry that she could still flatter me, that I still cared so much about her opinion.

I was suited up, the brown fabric covering me like a second skin. She stared me down, watching me hungrily. Like my hips, my skin, my blood she wanted more than food, than air itself. For what it's worth, Isis had plenty game. I didn't want to play anymore.

I no longer welcomed her visits.

"Na-Na."

I didn't answer. Walked off the set, manually raised the lights in the cave. No illusions now. Just the truth. My heart rate skyrocketed. Management monitoring me could tell I was about to bust a gut. The cave suddenly filled with the hiss of fresh oxygen.

"Sanaa?"

I turned from my wet bar, nothing fancy, just aloe juice and wheatgrass shots and whatever "proprietary" ingredients they stashed in the energy blasts. The nasty taste, like much of my life in the cave, I had long gotten used to.

Isis had completely shaved her head. Only a little blond stubble, her new growth, was visible, and the tell-tale tiny cuts on her scalp where Management had implanted receptor nanitic sensors designed to perfectly map the incoming kinematic data onto her own motor cortex. The old scars still looked like angry red ants. Unlike the dark interface nodes that dotted my spine and every limb. I realized I had never seen the real Isis or her natural hair. When we first met in Goat Park she was rocking a red afro and Bootsy shades. She looked like Little Orphan Annie and the Mack. I must have looked at her like I was crazy, but how could I not be? I had wanted to be a dancer, but now nearly all of my flesh sang the body electric. Mite-sized robots, nanites interfacing directly with the motor neurons along my spine and limbs, translated my subtlest intentions, the bioelectrical precursors to thought and will, into movement data. Management's distributed processing network instantly transferred this kinematic stream via encrypted, high-bandwidth satellite uplinks that downloaded it to Isis, wherever she was in the empire star. The system even learned, subtly reinforcing movements which garnered the biggest audience response data, sometimes making my own body feel fractionally alien to me. My dance became Isis's own. An interstellar duet, imperceptible to the media or her global fans, we were captives of the flame.

And zeros or not, I was losing, had lost nearly everything.

When my nana died, Management would not let me go to the funeral. I was furious. Trapped in the crystal cave, I raged for days until my body was spent. Isis was scheduled to perform at a major, international awards show. I could not be spared. The satellites watched over both of us, no matter how far apart we were, no matter how much I grieved. Despair filled my crystal cave.

Sometimes I wondered if the nanites weren't subtly pruning neural pathways not related to dance, optimizing their host, erasing the unnecessary baggage of memory.

The fragile peace of the crystal cave splintered as Isis broke the silence.

"Oh, this," she said and raked freshly manicured pointed nails across her crown. Her fingertips looked like daggers. Manicurists and stylists were sent to me each week, but I kept my nails, my hair simple. Who would ever see me?

"Management wanted me to cut it," she said. "They won't tell me yet what they're going to do to my hair. You know them. Always got some next level plan for me to take over. First music, then the world." She laughed carefree, the way only white girls could, and walked over to me. She smelled like roses, or was it that flower my nana used to wear, the one in her garden. I had to work harder and concentrate to remember, to hold on to where my family and I used to live. To remember their faces, and the foods we used to eat, my friends, Bijou, Chanel, even the fine boys in the park, everyone that Management paid off long ago so they would forget me. I was losing parts of my memory, losing parts of myself.

I couldn't believe I used to love her.

"We are like this," Isis said. She grasped my hands, formed a knot. "Sacred. Nothing is more sacred than sisters, than the bond we have."

I wanted to cry, but I was too exhausted. Did she even care that I no longer remembered my sisters' names?

"I love the new choreography, love it! Girl, you're brilliant! With it, there is *no way* we can't make history. Not this time. We're selling out everywhere, and I mean everywhere. So you can't leave now. You can retire later but not now, Sanaa. And you know I love you."

Why it got to be like this, I wanted to know. Why can't nobody want me, all of me, just as I am? I used to have that, didn't I? I couldn't remember. I let go. Her hands felt clammy, cold, inhuman. I didn't want to be near her anymore. We were close enough.

If she noticed my distaste, Isis was too professional to let on. I'm sure Management had given her a script. Isis was good at memorizing her lines. She lip-synced better than anyone who ever lived.

"Got somethin' for ya." She handed me a box.

Ksst. I didn't want any more payoffs from her, no more expensive trinkets and souvenirs. What was the use when I no longer had a life?

"Go 'head, open it," she commanded. There was the Isis I knew. I snatched it from her open palm.

"I don't need your toys, Ice, I need my freedom."

I tossed the velvet ribbon and opened the latch. A gold and diamond encrusted ankh decorated with a scarab beetle rested on a white satin lotus flower.

"Thanks." I walked away. I needed to shower, to sleep before the next rehearsal. It was obvious that neither Isis nor Management cared about me. Something about geese and golden eggs.

As I turned the lights back off, I could see Ice's face before she slipped out the door. If I didn't know better I would have sworn she was crying.

"Keep it," she said before the cave sealed me in. "I have one, too. Just like it. You might need it one day."

Something about the way she said that, no hustle, no hype, made me shiver. I walked back from the sauna room and into the main set, raised the lights. The crystal cave hummed quietly. The big screens were turned to saver mode. Pictures of the past tour dates flickered by. Barcelona, Rome, Munich, Istanbul,

Amsterdam, places I might never live to see. So why would I need a gaudy necklace, even if it was worth two mints?

I picked the box off the floor and examined it. A typical jewelry gift box, plush, expensive looking. I flipped it open, pulled out the cross-like ankh. I was offended because it was like something Isis's press crew would hand out in swag bags. Besides the crap ton of diamonds, nothing special. Or was it?

"Music: Ndegeocello, 'Dance of the Infidel,'" I said. Light trumpets and jazz drifted through the air. I set the box down on a coffee table and sank into the couch in the rear of the cage. The seat cushions molded themselves around my body, enveloping me like a cozy cocoon. The amulet was expertly made, heavily encrusted with jewels. But it wasn't the jewels Isis wanted me to see. There was something beyond them. Something extra that she hadn't wanted Management to know.

I traced my fingertips along the curves of the ankh, then noticed that the largest diamond was in the center, below the scarab. I stroked it with my thumb, then pressed down hard. To my surprise, the amulet broke apart. My left hand held the bottom of the cross, and in my right was the top of the golden bow with the scarab beetle. I held the dagger in my trembling hand and sank deeper into the couch.

The blade was sharp, lethal enough to pierce skin, slash arteries. Ice had said she had one of these, too. Was that her retirement plan all along?

I rejoined the ankh, held it by its glittering bow, placed it carefully on the table. They said the dragon can't dance. I always thought that wasn't true. Looking in the mirror that was my crystal cave, I didn't know anymore. But the blade's cool weight in my palm hummed with a different kind of truth, a silent choreography yet to unfold.

Rafters Hold

"Not a house in the country ain't packed to its
rafters with some dead Negro's grief."
—Toni Morrison, *Beloved*

These walls   breathe it slow
inhale   exhale   sorrow dust   Plaster sighs fine powder   coats the
tongue   tastes metal   river mud   Every nail hammered through a
name   forgotten   every joist a bone   settling   The house holds echo
Whip sound   quick   sharp   Chain sings low   misery tune   hymns
hold the quiet   after after after the breaking

Rafters groan low   swing by and hear   Not age   not weather alone
This weight   unseen   pressing down   This weight bearing Grief dense
a humid season   trapped inside   Thick on window glass   a film
Makes floorboards whisper   keen   underfoot

Milk ghost   still stains the air   Stolen   spilled   refused   Baby teeth gone
to water   gone to iron   Rememory blooms   chokecherry tree   carved raw
on a bent black back   Its bitter flower   falls   seeds grief   in floor cracks

Ohio water remembers   holds breath   holds bodies   But won't hold
justice Mud banks keep secrets   dark   suck down screams   Refuse

forgetting   Spit back daughters   dripping   water weed wet   hungry
consuming   light

This country   damn the foundation built   on that packed earth grief
that burial ground   raked by thieves   Rafters   beams   cornerstones
Negro sorrow   load bearing   structural anomalies   my timbers ache
holds   mounds of lore
the painted red-lipped smile   holds the muffled scream   holds the long lie
masking truth   holds the crushing   weight   of   every   broken   child
holds you   now   listening

Child's Play

SHE PUT THE GLOVES on each hand and let the clear plastic snap back around her wide, brown wrists. It startled Her, popped and hummed, like when the first star blew nova. These were long-fingered, big boned hands, wide in the center, strong, generous. God found that She liked them, and it was good. She let the dry, smooth powdery sensation of the gloves sink into this new skin. Funny, She always forgot what it was like to slip into the cells and membranes, the blood and bone of these Living. It too was a humming, a hymn really, a kind of cellular symphony that reminded Her of why She'd made these Living most like kin.

She listened through Willie Mae's inner ear, Willie Mae who lived in a treeless shotgun house on Randle Street in North Memphis, Willie Mae who worked as a lunch lady in a charter school shoehorned into another school. God listened and heard the curious contralto of the women's voices. Their laughter tickled the inside of Her, made her want to add this one's voice to the song. God wondered what its key was.

"They think they the only ones run things. Don't they know we got power, too? Try to put some tired, gray, mushy broccoli on them trays, and let them take one bite. *One*. That child will never eat broccoli again. *Ever*. Not for their whole life," Ira Lee, the other Living one said, her eyes wide as a 12-quart pot. "Not one piece, long as they live, and breathe, and walk God's green earth."

"Child, I told you that one was crazy," Willie Mae said, nodding at a young woman's retreating back. "Always pushing through the line. Can't wait her turn, knocking the poor children over, and can't even speak."

"How they s'posed to learn about manners if they own teacher ain't got none?"

"That's what I'm saying. Children learn what you show them, not that foolishness grown folks say but never do."

"Amen," God said, and it was good. *Amen, Amen, Amen.* This one's voice! It reminded her of that other Living, the one that lived not so long ago. She had been singing since she was . . . what would this one say? God stretched and yawned, reached into the wet, webbed electric lines of the Living's memory. What was that word, how would she say it here? Yes! She had been singing since she was a *little bitty baby, not even knee high to a duck.* A duck! God chuckled, and it was good. She liked how this one spoke, how all the Living in this part of the great, wide world turned the Word on its head and made others listen with another ear. Willie Mae was no Mahalia, nor no Bessie neither, but God could hear some of the same genius genes *hymnsinging* in the woman's blood. God wondered if the lunch lady knew she could sing, *sang* as they said around these parts. God wondered if she wanted to. God wasn't sure if Willie Mae, who had stood in size ten, padded Hush Puppy shoes for fifteen years in the kitchen of Scenic Hills Elementary, *Bobcats, go!*, this lunch lady who fed a whole generation of Memphis City Schools students, but had no children of her own, God wondered if she even wanted to sing. Did Willie Mae enjoy music? God shifted inside the Living's skin and sent a tiny, electric pulse in through the backdoor of this one's memory rooms. Later, much later, perhaps a new cell would form and grow, multiplying and dividing until a new thought was had. Maybe. God wasn't sure, and see, that's the part some of the Living got wrong.

She wasn't omnipotent, all knowing. At least not anymore. Over millennia upon millennia, Her memory had begun to fail. Or more specifically, She'd loosened her grip, let the rope and its myriad threads hang lax in Her great, gifting hands. The details, all the many-layered membranes, the labyrinth electric lines of possibility had stretched and yawned over the pulse of time. She'd let them wander in and out of Her thoughts, let them twist and turn upon themselves until sometimes She was as addled and unsure as the eldest elder, navigating between the Past, the Present, and the Part to Be, the Part that Could Be—if.

Like now. One temple faced the faded "Milk Does the Body Good" sign and the other was turned against the "Power of the Pyramid" poster on her right, but this *dang, Dang!* mandatory plastic cap dug into her crown and her forehead, made her whole brain ache. And it did not take God to know that a migraine headache was no good. The ill-fitting cap made her head ache so that she could not remember the parts of the recipe. Neither God nor Willie Mae could remember if the recipe called for two parts relish and one part celery, or if it was two parts celery and one part relish. God relaxed and let the Living take a moment to sort it out. She liked how this one's mind moved through its problems, a most unusual thinker. This one took the parts of her problems and lifted them up like different colored squares in a great, big ole crazy quilt. She turned the thoughts around in her mind, thirty degrees to the left, forty-five degrees to the right, *indigo, cobalt*, no, *haint* blue fabric flipped this way, and *Red Banks, Mississippi* red that other way. God floated inside a cool, shady corner of the lunch lady's mind, sat and rocked a while in a great, comfy chair. The woman's thoughts blew past Her, welcoming as a river breeze. Willie Mae's thoughts shimmered and swayed as if to say, *"Come on in and rock a while. I have so much I must tell You."*

Willie Mae took the great glass bowl in her left hand, a giant silver spoon in her right. She mixed the tuna in brisk, bold, deliberate circles, *whomp*. The flesh on the woman's great arms shook and swayed, *whomp*, like a lazy comet's tail or an eight-year-old's snake hips in a hand-me-down hula hoop, *whomp*, *whomp*. The lunch lady's underarm flab jerked and hooked in a slow, elliptical motion. God relished this and rippled pleasure, the great eye of a hurricane. And it was good, so very good. Problem solved, haint blue and red banks now blended into a prayerful purple. The rocking stopped. God sat still, wrapped in a patch quilt of thought, humbled by this Living one and even a little afraid.

In the stillness, She remembered why She had come here. Why she rocked inside a woman who was more at home in this school cafeteria kitchen than she ever was in her empty house on Randle Street with its mesh screen doors and storm glass windows mosquitoes still managed to get through. God remembered why She returned to the Living that She had made, why She explored the playgrounds of their unusual minds. It was always this unpredictableness, this universal element of surprise. She liked how the wise ones followed their first instincts. The recipe! It was indeed two parts relish and one part celery. The children would love it, but something was missing. The lunch lady and God sent out tiny tendrils of thought.

Of all God's gifts, She coveted nothing more than onions. *Hmmmm*, these She could not resist. What recipe for tuna fish salad could be complete without some relish—sweet if you could get it—some celery, some juicy boiled eggs, garlic salt, a dash of mustard, real mayonnaise—none of that "whip" stuff, God liked real mayo, God didn't like ugly—and a healthy dose of the sweetest, crispest white onions? The lunch lady's full lips smiled. *And since She was up South, in the land of the tastiest, why not indulge in a bit of pecans. Wouldn't sprinkling in a few of them make the tuna salad quite perfect, even more irresistible, delightful, beyond special?*

Pecans?

Willie Mae frowned, her great, gifting, skilled hand poised above the kitchen knife. It hovered above the neat pile of pecans, as if they were the wrong key on a grand piano. *Pecans? Nuts? In her mama's tuna fish salad? Might as well put raisins in chicken salad!* God felt the lunch lady's thoughts ripple, rumble even, the first thundered warning of a summer storm, resistance.

No one put nuts in tuna salad, and if one did, if one was odd enough, walnuts might do. But pecans? Pecans belonged in pie. Everybody on God's green earth knew that. Great, sticky slices of pecan pie with golden honey and maple syrup, sweet and pure. God settled back in the rocking chair, chuckled and waited. She let Willie Mae's thoughts jump and tumble. Resistance whacked the pine floorboards of the woman's mind. An infinite hum buzzed between the turning ropes, like the old General Electric fan that whirred lazily on the canned goods shelf. The sound alternated between the consequences and the possibilities; a Double Dutch rhythm beat inside God's inner ear. She waited and listened, while the woman wrestled within herself, then Willie Mae dropped the doubled ropes. Her resolve rang out loud and clear.

And that was another thing the Living got wrong. God was neither the turner of the jump ropes, nor the jumper. She was the turner, and the jumper, and the doubled ropes that hit the pavement and the rhythm in between. She was all this and nothing. She could change the time, call out for a new rhyme, but in the end, She was the ripple of air that sang and hummed beneath the Living's jumping feet. Sometimes the spirit soared, flawless, formless in the air, and sometimes the spirit faltered, stumbled, and tripped over the twin ropes—and missed a beat. It was not God's place to choose the rhythm of the game, but only to maintain the music. She set the heart in motion, but it was not She who chose its lifelong rhythm or how it pumped and if or how the Living danced to the beat.

Willie Mae shook and nodded her head, while God sat in the corner of her mind and rocked quietly, tapped a restless foot. Finally the seesaw settled with a loud *thud.* The merry-go-round ceased its endless squeaking and spinning. Haint blue blended with Mississippi red. Willie Mae scooped the pile of pecans in her great brown hand, scooped them like a handful of jacks or the newborn, dying stars God had scattered across the universe.

"Willie Mae, what you doin'?" Ira Lee asked. God heard the name and the tentative, nameless tune that escaped from Willie Mae's lips, and it was good. God clapped Her hands like a small child, rested them in Her billowy lap.

"Nothing." Willie Mae the lunch lady took the knife and *chopped, chopped, chopped* and diced the pecans into tiny bits of brown dust, so small an eye could barely see them. She then scooped them in the palm of her hand and sprinkled them in the great glass bowl of tuna. She took a finger, wrapped in plastic, and spooned out a taste. *Hmmmm.* God sighed inside her. The tuna salad now complete, she covered it. The aluminum foil crinkled and crackled beneath her heavy hands. The lunch lady hummed a lilting little tune to herself, quiet and shy at first; then her voice rang out bold and joyful as a rising sun. Willie Mae rested the bowl on a shelf. She gently closed the refrigerator. Her padded size tens seemed to glide and dance across the checkered linoleum floor. God rocked and waited inside, silent as a womb.

The next day, Willie Mae adjusted the plastic cap that covered the white, spirally curls atop her head. She would have preferred a hair net, but don't get her started talking about how they run down the public schools. The elastic snapped and popped her temples, etched a groove in her forehead. She adjusted it again. The tight band was giving her one hell of a headache.

"You a'ight?" Ira Lee asked and tied her Memphis City Schools apron straps twice around her wide, lumpy waist.

"Yeah," Willie Mae said and placed a few more empty trays on the counter.

"Girl, you put yo' foot in that tuna salad."

"Thank you." Willie Mae let the compliment ease the crick in her neck and whistled a few more notes from her strange, new tune. Comfortable now, she watched the first classroom of children clamor into line. They shouted and poked each other. They tried to skip, and when caught, scurried back and giggled into place. They traded insults and tossed jokes and dented cartons of chocolate milk as they did each day. The teacher, *Ms. Thang*, as Ira Lee called her, sashayed in line in a bright and beautiful, tight-fitting floral. This dress was new. All of Ms. Thang's dresses were new. Ms. Thang never wore the same dress on any given day. She tossed shiny, brown hair over thin, stooped shoulders and elbowed one or two of the third graders, as she bulldozed her way through the line. She carried her tray high above her head, stiff-armed like a University of Memphis running back or that cross-bearing Statue of Liberty over on Mendenhall and Mt. Moriah.

Ms. Thang did not speak.

Ira Lee shot her an evil eye and Willa Mae's apron shook as she laughed. When the child Sabra came, pony tail turned lopsided, the great black, wiry afro puff leaning in the heat and the humid air, Willie Mae felt sorrow in the back of her belly. This one had great round eyes, big and shiny as the cat eye marbles Willie Mae had collected when *she* was a little girl. And a way about her, a tremble and a shake that made Willie Mae think of a frightened bird, like the ones long ago, cornered by that mangy stray cat in her Uncle Juicy's old orchards that became shotgun houses, and the shotgun houses that became high-end condos. Willie Mae grabbed the silver spoon and gave the great glass bowl a big dip.

"Here, child," she said. "Something extra for somebody special."

Sabra gave her a quick, dimpled smile, polite and furtive.

To Willie Mae, the smile was like the sun that peeked from behind a cloud and hid again. The girl moved slowly, head bowed, through the line. Sabra did not tell the nice lunch lady that she did not like tuna. She did not tell the nice lunch lady that she never ate it. But something, a little tickle in the temple above her right ear, made the child take a scoop with her chubby finger. Something made her scoop it up, made her pop it right in her snaggle-toothed mouth. Hmmm, the tuna was good. Real good. What had the nice lunch lady said? *Something special for somebody extra?* No. *Something extra for somebody special.* Yes. That was right. Gold star for Sabra! The nice lunch lady had called her *special.* Sabra was special. Sabra liked how the lunch lady had looked at her. Like she really was special. A real good girl and not somebody nasty. Not like Ms. Whittle looked at her, like she was somebody poor, like she was somebody everybody should feel sorry for.

There were three Jaylens spelled three different ways in Ms. Whittle's third grade class. Sabra waited in line behind Jaylen Number Three when the first hiccup hit her. Sabra's belly bounced and lurched, leapt up and down like a basketball before the tuna bounced from her belly and raced through her neck, tumbled past her tongue and slid over her teeth. Sabra shook, and her cat marble eyes spun in her head as the plastic tray with the tuna and sweet green peas and the carton of chocolate milk and her spork spilled onto the linoleum floor. She was falling when she heard Ms. Whittle scream and the lunch ladies cry, "Somebody get her! She's fallen!"

Two, four, six, eight warm, strong hands grabbed and held her up. Sabra heard Jaylen Number Three call her name, heard the children's high-pitched screams, like Ms. Whittle's loud whistle at recess when it was time to line up, time to go back in. Sabra felt dizzy, couldn't feel her toes. Her throat seized up on her, like when she sucked chocolate milk through a straw. Her skin felt hot and swollen. She could not breathe and for a moment Sabra felt like one of those red balloons that swell and blow up, the ones UniverSoul circus clowns twisted into puppies and princesses for the kids who'd had spending money on that third grade field trip. Then Sabra didn't hear anymore, then Sabra didn't think anymore, at least not for a second. Another retch tumbled and shook inside. Her body quaked, tectonic shocks of tuna spilled down her crimson and navy blue plaid dress, ruined her, down, down to the shiny tips of her patent leather Mary Jane shoes.

Inside Sabra, God rocked and waited. She swung back and forth on a tiny wooden plank held by two great ropes. She listened for the *hum-hum-hymning* sound of the child's fretful breathing. She waited and wondered if this Living one would be alright, a'ight. She waited and wondered until She heard the EMT grunt and snort. He muttered a curse, held the child in his arms, gentle, real gentle, like a limp, black baby doll. God rocked and waited as the tearful teacher mumbled something about "an allergy to nuts." God rocked and waited as the school nurse cried, "anaphylactic shock." God waited until She felt the sharp needle's sting, quick as a cottonmouth's bite.

God tucked in Her knees, swung back real wide then jumped inside the EMT and listened as he muttered his litany of prayers. The siren blasted as the bus sped down Scenic Highway, turned on two wheels off Walnut Road, hopscotched through traffic. God waited as the EMT called on Elegbá. He wiped his smooth, hairless head and held the little girl's hand. Bright blue and gold bead necklaces swung on his neck, tangled in a heavy black rope dangling with keys. The young man's prayers alternated between Cuban Spanish and English, sprinkled with the seeds of an ancient language God recognized as one of Her many names. God listened to the man's prayer and it was good. *God bless the child, God save and protect the child, God don't let this little girl die on my shift, shit, God, please.* She waited inside him and swung Her legs until, prayer ended, the child delivered, they both heard the doctor's gasp when she examined the child in the Emergency Room.

God pumped Her legs, threw back Her great lolling head, until the doctor waved at a weary nurse in violet scrubs and brand new shoes, until the weary nurse called for the social worker and the social worker stroked the child's wiry curls that sprouted, thick and puffy around her temples, stroked her as she cried and snotted, whispered then sang a song of unbroken blues, until the social worker closed the door behind her, let out a heavy sigh, plopped down in a warped wheeled chair, and picked at the dirt beneath purple painted nails as she whispered in the phone, *hush, hush, hush,* to the school principal.

God waited and rocked, rocked and waited until She heard the school principal slowly, punch out the rhythm of 9-1-1, rocked and waited for the beep that would bring the police out to the elementary school on the hill. And God waited until She heard the mother's sharp cry as she collapsed, a broken pile upon the hospital's shiny floor. God waited until the father fell, in slow motion, like a great building imploding, in disbelief, waited as he wailed the name of the family friend who broke sacred trust, the name of the man who ground a small girl's innocence in the dust. God kicked Her feet, *pumped, pumped* Her square knees and took a great deep breath. Waited until She could hear no more, until She could feel no more, until She was certain the child would be in harm's way no more. God closed Her eyes, threw back Her great head, gave Her legs one last big *pump*, then released the swing's heavy ropes, and leapt back into the universe.

Conjuring Legacies

The Saar Women's Reclamation of History, Identity, and the Black Spiritual Tradition

"Oh, how the signs obscure true knowledge and I am blazed
In this dark room, hungry, cold and searching—who is this thief
And why has she cast this curse . . ."
—Patricia Spears Jones, "Betye Saar's 'Mystic
Chart for an Unemployed Sorceress'"

Bearing the weight and length of the name "Mystic Chart for an Unemployed Sorceress" within its title, Jones's beautiful poem resonates with a feeling of growing irrelevance and a poignant search for meaning in a complex world. This sentiment echoes through the art of the Saar women, whose creations often feel like a brave deciphering of history, an excavation of identity, and a quest for understanding within the "dark room" of societal injustice and personal struggle. The Saar women's art aligns with womanist Afrofuturism, a vibrant framework that merges Black feminist thought with radical speculative imagination and a deep investigation of spirituality to explore the past, present, and future of Black women. This perspective is rooted in womanism, a term coined by Alice Walker to articulate a Black feminist consciousness. Walker defined womanism as a philosophy that centers Black women's experiences, celebrates their culture, and acknowledges the intersecting oppressions of race and gender. It is an understanding of the interconnectedness of gender and race, a recognition that the struggle for liberation is a shared one—a fabric composed from the threads of many voices—and directly addresses the unique challenges and lived experiences of Black women, specifically in contrast to traditional, white-centered feminist approaches.

Womanist Afrofuturism, building on this foundation, employs speculative and visionary modes to not only critique existing power structures but also to imagine and enact liberatory alternatives. This approach finds powerful echoes in the literary tradition, echoing the world-building survival strategies of figures like Lauren Olamina in Octavia E. Butler's best-selling *Parable* series and the reclaiming of ancestral power central to works by authors such as Andrea Hairston and Nalo Hopkinson. Importantly, for the Saars, neither womanism nor feminism functions as a rigid dogma or an overarching force shaping their artistic expression; instead, their work embodies an inherent understanding of these interconnected principles.

These artists are dangerous muses, challenging established narratives and societal expectations. They are "dangerous" not because they are malicious, but because their creative visions disrupt oppressive systems and (re)construct identities, histories, and futures. Butler's character Lauren Olamina perfectly embodies this "dangerous muse" archetype as both creator and visionary; she literally *conjures* a new religion, Earthseed, and a path forward from societal collapse, grounded in radical empathy and a clear-eyed view of change. This fictional act of world-building from the fragments of the present resonates with the Saars' own artistic practices—their creation of new meaning from discarded objects, their focus on resilience, and their commitment to shaping futures through a visionary lens.

The Saar women, like other Black women speculative artists, embody this possibility and wield the power of reclamation, reinterpretation, and visionary storytelling to center Black women's experiences, reclaim marginalized histories, and conjure empowering narratives that reach across time and space.

#

On an unknown day, the sun spills through the windows of Betye Saar's studio, illuminating a constellation of found objects, each one a relic of a life lived, a whisper of a story waiting to be told. Here, in this sanctuary of memory and imagination, Betye Saar, the matriarch, the spinner of dreams, conjures magic from the mundane, her hands transforming the discarded into the divine. "My greatest pleasure," she says, guiding viewers of her online MOMA studio tour, "is just to walk around this space and move things and adjust things until a little piece develops. It's sort of like play." Her assemblages, like altars to the ancestors, hold the weight of history, the ache of injustice, and the defiant resilience of the Black spirit. A weathered window frame, its paint peeling like old wounds, becomes a portal to a young girl's dreams. The girl's silhouette is a shadow dancing in the moonlight, surrounded by a constellation of talismans—a crescent moon, a tattered playing card, a faded photograph—each one a verse in the poem of her life. This is *Black Girl's Window* (1969), a love letter to Black girlhood, a testament to the dreams that take root in the fertile soil of imagination.

Aunt Jemima, once a symbol of servitude, her smile a mask hiding generations of pain, is reborn in Betye Saar's hands in *The Liberation of Aunt Jemima* (1972). Here she stands, fist raised in defiance, a rifle in her hands, a Black Power fist blazing where the handkerchief once bound. This is not the Aunt Jemima of pancake boxes and subservience. This is a warrior queen, a goddess of liberation, her eyes burning with the fire of righteous anger. This piece, a revolutionary act of defiance, was hailed by Angela Davis as the revolutionary spark that ignited the Black women's movement—a recognition Betye Saar called "a real thrill" in her 2016 *Frieze* essay where she discusses her influences. This reclamation of Aunt Jemima, transforming her into a powerful symbol of resistance, aligns with the core tenets of womanist Afrofuturism. It demonstrates the dangerous muse in action, challenging the racist and sexist narratives embedded in popular culture and offering a Black woman-centered vision of empowerment. By arming the ubiquitous Aunt Jemima figure, Saar reclaimed history for Black women not only in America but also for those around the world who have been instrumental in both war and freedom movements.

Betye's art speaks in a language of symbols, a visual incantation. The celebrated artist's work is a conjure woman's spell that bends the arc of history towards justice. "I am a maker of objects," she proclaims, pointing the viewers' eyes to numerous eclectic found objects that comprise her assemblage collage. "I will go to a flea market or a thrift store or an antique store and just wait for an inspiration to come from an article that I find." She is a griot in three dimensions, her work a testament to the enduring power of Black history to shape the present and conjure the future.

And within this legacy of powerful creations, there exists a throne, not of gold or jewels, but of salvaged memories and ancestral dreams. *Ancestral Spirit Chair* (1992), residing in the hallowed halls of Smith College, is a testament to Betye Saar's ability to transmute the discarded into the divine, to evoke magic from the remnants of the past. Imagine a chair birthed from the earth's womb, its back a gnarled tapestry of branches reaching skyward like the arms of a supplicant, adorned with a constellation of glass bottles that shimmer like captured stars, each one holding the echo of a forgotten dream. Bits of mirror, reflecting shattered histories, fragments of bone, the echoes of ancestors long gone, and rusted metal, the scars of a nation's sins, are integrated into its form, a chorus of voices singing the song of survival.

It is a seat of power and prophecy, sacred and mundane, art and functional. A throne fit for an African queen, a goddess descended from the stars, or perhaps the ancestors themselves. Their spirits are infused into the very fabric of the chair. The throne invites us to sit and bear witness to the enduring spirit of Black history, to the stories etched in the lines of our hands, the rhythms that pulse in our blood. It appears designed to seat divinity, royalty, a child, or ancient African fae.

This evocative sculpture draws inspiration from the Kongo tradition of glass bottle trees, where vessels are hung on limbs like offerings to the spirits. These bottle trees are believed to capture and contain spirits, both benevolent and malevolent. This spiritual practice, carried across the ocean in the souls and minds of enslaved Africans, found new life in the Caribbean and the American South. There, bottle trees still stand as sentinels, silent guardians of homes and communities, their branches reaching towards the heavens like the great arms of a prayer, expressing the encoded memory and longing of enslaved Africans. That such cultural seeds would take root in various forms, like the reverence for blue bottles in 1790s Jamaican obeah folk magic, reminds us that the human desire to connect to the divine remains intact despite adversity.

As Robert Farris Thompson notes in his seminal work *Flash of the Spirit: African and Afro-American Art and Philosophy* (1983), these practices represent a continuity of African spiritual traditions. They are a testament to the resilience and adaptability of Black culture in the face of forced migration and cultural erasure—a chorus of survival and resistance that echoes across eras and geographies.

Betye Saar's chair becomes a potent vessel holding the collective imprint of the diasporic journey and enduring African spiritual memory. This connection between African spiritual practices and their retention and survival in the diaspora, transmuted into powerful artistic expression, speaks directly to the heart of Womanist Afrofuturism. It illustrates how the Saars, like many Black women artists, draw upon ancestral knowledge and spiritual traditions to reclaim their heritage and create a future where these traditions thrive. In doing so, they embody the dangerous muse, channeling the wisdom of the past to empower the present and shape the future. This enduring connection across the Atlantic, this insistence on memory as a source of power, resonates profoundly with Betye Saar's career-long engagement with the legacy of enslavement. As scholar Celeste-Marie Bernier discusses regarding Saar's pivotal *Diaspora* installation, Saar confronted the visual representation of the Middle Passage directly, recognizing its lasting trauma. Saar herself articulated the indelible nature of this history after incorporating a slave ship diagram into the work, concluding: "It would never wear out, because that slave ship imprint is on all of us. It is there forever! And it is also on the imprint of white Americans, too." This inescapable "slave ship imprint," Bernier argues, becomes a dominant symbol in Saar's visual lexicon. The recognition of this shared, persistent legacy underscores the historical consciousness that grounds and inspires the Saar women's artistic practice.

As Betye Saar writes in her poem "Diaspora" (1992):

> Seek the dark corner of the Ancestral Chair,
> Breathe on the embers of Africa
> and Recall the memory of fire.

Betye Saar's installations and sculptures as well as her small, potent assemblages are clearly created in synchrony with the Afrofuturist concept of encoding powerful messages and spiritual technologies within seemingly mundane objects. It transforms the concept of the box into a vessel of ancestral power, a microcosm of the larger themes of reclamation and resistance that run through the Saar women's work.

Betye Saar's *Gris-Gris Box* uses the imagery of ritual and protection, central to many African spiritual traditions, to create a space of empowerment and agency, particularly for Black women who have historically been denied both. Malcolm X said,

> The most disrespected person in America is the Black woman.
> The most unprotected person in America is the Black woman.
> The most neglected person in America is the Black woman.

In *Gris-Gris Box* (1985), a weathered wooden box, no bigger than a heart's desire, becomes a sanctuary, a haven for the spirit. Inside, a tiny figure kneels, surrounded by protective charms and talismans, invoking the power of ancestral spirits, a prayer whispered in the darkness, a plea for guidance and protection. This harnessing of Betye Saar's mojotech, spiritual technology within a contained object, is a powerful, intentional act of conjure. Betye Saar's art finds literary kinship in the worlds of Andrea Hairston, notably in novels like *Redwood and Wildfire* and *Will Do Magic for Small Change*. Her characters deploy performance—theatre, music, stage magic—intertwined with deeply rooted hoodoo knowledge as vital tools. In the hands of the masterful author, these are not mere entertainments, but methods of protection, essential storytelling, and community survival crucial for navigating hostile histories and actively shaping alternative realities.

As the blues women who sang their sorrows and joys into the night, Betye Saar's found art sculptures embody a fierce passion, a refusal to be silenced. They are a reclamation of the body, a celebration of Black womanhood in all its complexity, a defiant cry against the forces that seek to confine and control. Betye Saar's art embodies this duality, this simultaneous embrace of vulnerability and strength, echoing the core of womanist Afrofuturism. Like a dangerous muse, she reclaims and celebrates the Black female form, refusing to allow it to be defined by the male gaze or the weight of historical oppression. Through an expansive, radical imaginative lens informed by a keen appreciation of history and power, Betye Saar reclaims the narrative of Black women's bodies, transforming them from sites of trauma into sources of strength and resilience. Her art celebrates their power, their beauty, and their evolving spirit, aligning perfectly with the core tenets of womanist Afrofuturism and the dangerous muse archetype.

This artistic command, a legacy of creative power, a conjure woman's birthright, flows through generations like a river of memory. It finds new expression in the hands of Betye Saar's three daughters, Alison Saar, Tracye Saar-Cavanaugh, and Lezley Saar, each one a vessel for the ancestral spirit, a conduit for the stories that yearn to be told.

Alison, with her breathtaking sculptures, gives form to the whispers of the past. Her gifted hands shape clay and wood into vessels that hold the weight of history and the lightness of dreams. Her figures, often monumental and nude, their bodies a testament to the power and beauty of Black womanhood, challenge the very notion of representation, defying the gaze that seeks to objectify and diminish. They are not simply bodies; they are the embodiment of a thousand stories, imbued with the strength and vulnerability of generations of Black women who have carried the world on their shoulders and still found the strength to sing. Alison Saar's sculptures, in particular, exemplify this dangerous muse archetype. Through her art, she reclaims and redefines the Black female form, challenging the objectification and silencing of Black women's bodies throughout history. Her works are in conversation with scholar Sakena Young-Scaggs's concept of "Ingathering"—a celebration of Black women's communal gathering that powerfully evokes shared experience and Spirit. This connection to a collective power, a shared spiritual and creative energy, is a recurring theme in Afrofuturist art, where the individual and the community are often intertwined in a dance of resistance and transformation.

Terra Rosa (1993), a life-sized pregnant woman sculpted from wood and coated in red earth, her belly a vessel of life and legacy, sits with her heart exposed, a symbol of both vulnerability and strength. Here, Alison Saar employs the Afrofuturist trope of reimagining the body, and fertility, as a source of power and resilience. The red earth evokes a connection to ancestral lands and the lifeblood of generations, while the exposed heart speaks to the courage and vulnerability inherent in the act of creation. This image directly challenges historical and contemporary attempts to control and exploit Black women's bodies, presenting instead a vision of strength and self-determination rooted in ancestral power and connection to the earth. It symbolizes the power of creation and the enduring legacy of motherhood. Beside her, a skeletal figure made of cotton, its hands stained red with the blood of ancestors, speaks to the brutal legacy of slavery, the ghosts that still haunt the American landscape. *Strange Fruit* (1995) depicts a woman hanging upside down, her body crafted from rusted tin. A haunting echo of the lynching tree evokes the horrors inflicted upon Black bodies, a stark reminder of the violence that has shaped the American story. Her work fits in the same scheme as the historical insights of Saidiya Hartman, particularly her books *Scenes of Subjection: Terror, Slavery, and Self-Making in Nineteenth-Century America* (1997) and *Lose Your Mother: A Journey Along the Atlantic Slave Route* (2007). These works, spun from the threads of history and memory, explore the complexities of Black history, motherhood, and identity, tracing the insidious legacy of slavery and its impact on the lives of Black women across generations, their voices echoing through time and space. This unflinching gaze at the brutal entanglement of history and the Black body resonates profoundly with the temporal and physical reckonings forced upon Dana in Octavia E. Butler's foundational time travel novel, *Kindred*, where the past refuses to remain buried, demanding to be felt and acknowledged.

And in *Snake Charmer* (1985), a woman, carved from wood and painted in earthy hues, her body a vessel of strength, stands with a serpent poised between her lips, its fangs glinting like secrets in the moonlight. The snake, its body a sinuous curve of bronze, a symbol of both danger and transformation, appears to dance with her, a duet of power and grace. This image, both alluring and unsettling, speaks to the duality of nature, the coexistence of darkness and light, the dance of life and death that shapes the human experience. This sculpture, later reimagined in the print, *Snake Man* (1994), captures the essence of Alison's artistic vision, her ability to transform found objects into potent metaphors that imbue the inanimate with spirit and meaning. Through this depiction, Alison Saar embodies the dangerous muse as a figure of primal power and transformative potential. The serpent, a recurring symbol in many African spiritual traditions, as Mami Wata, Damballah, and other divinities, suggests both danger and healing, and its dance with the woman represents a reclamation of agency and a communion with forces that transcend the ordinary.

With Alison Saar's alchemy, the kitchen shed its skin of simple domesticity, emerging as a sovereign territory. Here, the tools of sustenance—skillets, pots, spoons, washtubs—are reborn as instruments of defense, wielded by women turned warriors. Consider her *Kitchen Amazon*, cinched not in silk but in cast iron—a girdle of skillets. This deliberate armoring with domestic tools evokes a lineage of female power, perhaps recalling not only contested symbols like Hippolyta's magic girdle but also the potent authority signified by the regalia of African queen mothers or the fierce protective energy of warrior goddesses like Oya, reimagining everyday objects as emblems of sovereignty. Saar seizes these blended narratives, recasting the warrior queen within the domestic sphere, her skillets now gleaming symbols of dominion over a realm too often dismissed.

The very materials breathe history: repurposed ceiling tin carries the soft gleam of a naturally aged patina, echoing the time-worn whispers held within the vintage cloths she integrates into her companion paintings. As Betye Saar's daughter, Alison moves with an inherited understanding, a fluency in the language of assemblage learned at her mother's knee. The Saar women's sharing of knowledge is intergenerational and interdimensional. This artistic lineage fuels Alison's commitment to fusing found materials with potent storytelling. She doesn't just recycle objects; she resurrects mythologies like the best speculative artist, braiding their narrative strands with the tangible textures of the discarded to conjure fiercely womanist visions. It's a technique echoing the broader Afrofuturist practice of sampling the past—its textures, its stories, its spirits—to architect possibilities for a different tomorrow, a methodology reflective of how many Black creators engage with lineage and legacy.

Alison's decade-long *Skillet Studies* series is one of her greatest triumphs of reclamation and reimagination. In this powerful act, Alison transformed discarded cast-iron skillets, their surfaces blackened and rusted with the history of countless meals prepared and shared. Through her imagination, she turned cast-iron into canvases for her art, imbuing them with new life and meaning. This engagement aligns in spirit with some Afrofuturists' interest in reimagining the past and present through the lens of a bold imagination that serves as a possible catalyst for the future. Alison's reimagining of these classic symbols of domesticity offer a different perspective on the concept of comfort food and "curing." By repurposing cast-iron skillets and other throwaways, she elevates these undervalued tools of women's work to the realm of art and ritual. These once utilitarian objects, also symbols of enslaved, imprisoned domestic labor of Black women and the unseen hands that nourished generations, become vessels for Alison's vibrant cast iron portraits of Black women. She transforms them into canvases for the ethereal, creating what Young-Scaggs might term a "liminal space" where mundane objects fuel "life-giving endeavors." Their faces emerge from the darkness. Their eyes, painted in bold colors against the dark metal, meet the viewer with a gaze that demands recognition and respect. This act of reclamation speaks to Black women's ability to transmute the burdens of history into expressions of personal beauty and agency. In doing so they prove dangerous to the status quo, destroying the old temples of golden ages past, stealthily building the world anew in their own remarkable image. These works, this entire series, a tribute to the labor of Black women and girls, speaks to the importance of reclaiming narratives, of transforming the tools of domesticity into instruments of artistic expression, a defiant cry against the forces that seek to silence and erase. And the artistic legacy of Betye Saar, a mother's gift, a conjure woman's birthright, extends beyond Alison to encompass the creative expressions of her other daughters, Lezley Saar and Tracye Saar-Cavanaugh, each one a dream maker, a keeper of stories.

Lezley, a printmaker and mixed-media artist, explores the spaces where identity and representation blur. Her work speaks to the complexities of race, gender, and the body, infused with the power of magical realism. Like her solo show, *Madwoman in the Attic* (2019), a visual exploration of nineteenth-century Victorian literature, her art is a tribute to the women whose voices have been silenced, whose stories have been erased. It challenges traditional notions of beauty and power, reclaiming space for those who have been marginalized, whose experiences have been cast into the shadows.

In her *Gender Renaissance* series (2017–present), Lezley uses mixed-media portraits to explore the fluidity of gender, the dance of transformation, blurring the lines between male and female, human and animal, reality and fantasy. She invites us to question the very nature of identity. And in *A Conjuring of Conjurors* (2020), she creates an immersive installation of seven "shrines" dedicated to the ancestors, to the historical and fictional figures who embody resistance and survival, their spirits guiding us through the darkness. These figures, drawn from the wellspring of literature, mythology, and history, become totems of strength and inspiration, their eyes meeting ours across time and space, inviting us to connect with their stories, to draw power from their legacies.

Lezley Saar's work, like her mother's and sister's, often shares intrinsic traits with the Kongo concept of *minkisi,* transforming everyday objects and figures into vessels of spiritual power and ancestral memory. Within Lezley Saar's exhibit *Salon des Refusés* (Salon of the Rejected) (2017–2018), more recent constellations of her celebrated journey converge. The exhibition's name itself is an echo, a defiant resonance reaching back to Paris, 1863. There, artists shunned by the rigid pronouncements of the official Salon—a powerful arbiter of fame and oblivion—carved out their own space to be seen. Turned away for their unsettling aesthetics and their gaze fixed upon the commonplace rather than the anointed and the canonical, those nineteenth-century painters demanded their visions be witnessed. Lezley masterfully wields this historical echo as a metaphor, drawing a luminous line from those rejected canvases to the figures haunting her own portraits—individuals often relegated to the societal periphery, yet centered here with dignity and undeniable presence.

The task of chronicling and contextualizing this potent artistic lineage often falls to Tracye Saar-Cavanaugh, the family's insightful writer and photographer, and the manager for Betye Saar. Her contributions are crucial threads in their public presentation, appearing notably as essays in catalogues like *Family Legacies: The Art of Betye, Lezley, and Alison Saar* (2005) and the more recent exploration *Betye Saar: Extending the Table* (2023). It is often Tracye Saar-Cavanaugh's keen eye that frames intimate studio portraits or beautifully captures the intricate details of completed works, while her gifted hand pens reflections that guide our understanding of her siblings' and mother's. In the *Family Legacies* catalogue, for instance, she describes observing her mother and sisters as akin to "watching a magician practice her craft," highlighting the element of conjuring inherent in their art, and notes how Betye "recycles the spirits" of found objects.

Through her steady stewardship, Tracye Saar-Cavanaugh helps archive and interpret the story and legacy of her mother and sisters, as well as that of other visual artists whose work is conversation with the Saar women. The double and sometimes triple consciousness of the Saar daughters' work reflects the griotic gaze they share with each other and their fellow artist mother. To navigate the balance between personal biomythology, and formal art history and insight is no easy feat, particularly for one whose own story is connected by blood. It is a rare gift, then, to have one's creative artwork framed by someone you love and who is loved by you. Tracye Saar-Cavanaugh's dedicated work in documenting and interpreting the family's artistic output also embodies a form of spiritual and cultural preservation, akin to the power objects (the Kongo concept of minkisi) that hold ancestral knowledge.

As bell hooks reminds us in *Art on My Mind: Visual Politics* (1995), "art on the walls" can be a powerful tool for transformation, a way to challenge dominant narratives and create space for marginalized voices. The Saar women's work, with its focus on Black women's experiences and its reimagining and repurposing of discarded objects, embodies this transformative power, inviting us to reconsider the stories we tell ourselves about history, labor, and identity. Patricia Hill Collins's concept of intersectionality, which recognizes the complex interplay of race, gender, and class, provides a framework for understanding the layered meanings embedded in the family's art. And Audre Lorde's writings on the power of the erotic and the importance of self-expression mesh perfectly with the Saars' celebration of Black women's lives, their ability to find joy and beauty even in the midst of struggle.

The Saars' art, a disparate but connected chorus of voices rising in harmony, is undeniably rooted in the exploration of identity, but in nuanced and novel ways. Theirs is a multifaceted and ever-evolving concept, a journey of self-discovery that unfolds through layers of history, memory, and lived experience. For these women, being Black, being female, being artists—these are not separate categories but braided strands of their being, a testament to the complex and beautiful journey of Black womanhood. They embrace the complexities of their heritage, acknowledging the pain of racism and sexism, the wounds that have shaped their journeys, while celebrating the richness of their cultures, the strength of their ancestors, the enduring spirit that has carried them through the storm. Their art becomes a sanctuary, a space for self-discovery and healing, a place where they can explore the nuances of Black women's identities while giving voice to their own unique experiences, their unique visions emerging through the vagaries of the art world and society that might attempt to distort and limit them. This creative exploration extends beyond the personal, encompassing a broader understanding of Black identity in America, a collective experience shaped by history, memory, and the ongoing struggle for social justice.

And then there is the spiritual, the mystical, the unseen forces that permeate their work, the whispers of ancestors guiding their hands, the magic that flows through their veins. "I guess my work could be considered narrative because I feel that every object has its story about its previous life," Betye Saar reflects in her studio tour. "And sometimes I change that, but I like to have a lot unsaid so the viewer can kind of reinterpret what I'm trying to say." Betye Saar's fascination with hoodoo, with its roots in the soil of Africa, its branches reaching across the diaspora, adds another layer of meaning to her art. It is a dimension that transcends the physical, a connection to the spirit world. It's not just about history and identity; it's about the power of belief, the unwavering faith that has sustained Black people through centuries of struggle, the connection to the spiritual realm, the ancestral wisdom that guides and protects. Hoodoo, in the Saars' hands, becomes a tool for healing, a balm for the wounds of the past, a way to reclaim agency in the face of oppression. This spiritual dimension, a whisper in the wind, a flicker in the shadows, infuses their art with a sense of mystery, a sense of wonder, and a connection to something larger than themselves.

The Saars' artistic legacy reverberates with the ancestral memories of Black folklore and spiritual traditions. These cultural treasures add depth and complexity to the Saar women's visual narratives, their voices echoing through time and space. Betye Saar's work, a conjure woman's grimoire, often incorporates elements of mysticism and ritual, drawing inspiration from the African diasporic religions and practices that have sustained Black communities across the globe. Her installations become repositories of spiritual power, imbued with the energy of found objects, the whispers of ancestors, and the intentions of the artist. Her hands are a conduit for unseen forces that touch our lives.

In pieces like *Fertile Ground* (1993), a reflection on the act of creation and the complexity of motherhood, Alison Saar evokes the spirit of the earth, the fertile ground from which all life springs, and the evolving roles of women as creators and healers, their hands shaping the world, their voices sounding the songlines of existence. The Saars' art becomes a crossroads where the seen and unseen worlds converge, where history and spirituality intertwine, their voices blending in a chorus of ancestral memory, creating a visual language that speaks to the soul.

Central to this spiritual exploration, a pilgrimage to the heart of Blackness, is the recognition of African roots, the ancestral home that calls to us across the ocean, and the enduring legacy of traditions carried across the diaspora, the seeds of culture that have blossomed in new and unexpected ways. The Kongo concept of minkisi resonates through their work, a thread that connects them to the source. Betye Saar's assemblages, with their intricate layers of found objects and symbolic imagery, become vessels for minkisi, repositories of spiritual power that speak to the enduring connection between the physical and the spiritual realms. Alison's sculptures, with their evocative forms and symbolic references, also embody the spirit of minkisi, transforming the mundane into the magical, the everyday into the extraordinary. Lezley's mixed-media shrines and Tracye's archival work also, in their own ways, act as vessels or conduits for the minkisi principle—gathering fragments of memory and spirit to empower collective understanding and future vision.

In the light that streams through Betye Saar's studio, we see the transformative power of art. Its ability to heal and inspire, to conjure a world where Black voices resonate with the fullness of their humanity. Guided by their abundant curiosity and masterful skill, the art of the Saar women echoes through time and space. Their art leads us towards a future where their legacy will continue to uplift and illuminate. "I'm never out of ideas," Betye Saar declares, "and I think that's a good sign."

Works Cited

Anderson, Reynaldo. "Foreword: Contemporary Notes on the Black Speculative Arts Movement." *CLA Journal* 65, no. 1 (2022): 5–7.

Bernier, Celeste-Marie. "'The Slave Ship Imprint': Representing the Body, Memory, and History in Contemporary African American and Black British Painting, Photography, and Installation Art." *Callaloo* 37, no. 4 (2014): 990–1022. *Project MUSE*. https://doi.org/10.1353/cal.2014.0181.

Butler, Octavia E. *Kindred*. Beacon Press, 2003.

Butler, Octavia E. *Parable of the Sower*. Grand Central Publishing, 1993.

Collins, Patricia Hill. *Black Feminist Thought: Knowledge, Consciousness, and the Politics of Empowerment*. Hyman, 1990.

Dallow, Jessica, and Barbara C. Matilsky, editors. *Family Legacies: The Art of Betye, Lezley, and Alison Saar*. Ackland Art Museum, University of North Carolina at Chapel Hill / University of Washington Press, 2005.

Hairston, Andrea. *Redwood and Wildfire*. Aqueduct Press, 2011; Tor, 2022.

Hairston, Andrea. *Will Do Magic for Small Change*. Aqueduct Press, 2016; Tor, 2022.

Hartman, Saidiya. *Lose Your Mother: A Journey Along the Atlantic Slave Route*. Farrar, Straus, and Giroux, 2007.

Hartman, Saidiya. *Scenes of Subjection: Terror, Slavery, and Self-Making in Nineteenth-Century America*. Oxford University Press, 1997.

hooks, bell. *Art on My Mind: Visual Politics*. The New Press, 1995.

Jones, Patricia Spears. "Betye Saar's 'Mystic Chart for an Unemployed Sorceress.'" *The New Yorker*, November 30, 2020. https://www.newyorker.com/magazine/2020/11/30/betye-saars-mystic-chart-for-an-unemployed-sorceress.

Lorde, Audre. "Uses of the Erotic: The Erotic as Power." Delivered at the Fourth Berkshire Conference on the History of Women at Mount Holyoke College, August 25, 1978. Chap. 5 in *Sister Outsider: Essays and Speeches*. The Crossing Press, 1984.

Malcolm X. Speech. Los Angeles. May 22, 1962.

Marsh, Ariana, and Kat Widing. "20 Female Artists You Need to Know." *Harper's Bazaar*, May 30, 2020. https://www.harpersbazaar.com/culture/art-books-music/g7916/best-female-artists/.

Phillips, Layli. "Womanism: On its Own." In *The Womanist Reader: The First Quarter Century of Womanist Thought*, edited by Layli Phillips. Routledge, 2006, xix–lv.

Quallen, Brooklyn. "Who Is Sitting in 'Ancestral Spirit Chair'?" *SCMA Blog*, Smith College Museum of Art, January 24, 2023. https://scma.smith.edu/blog/who-sitting-ancestral-spirit-chair-0.

Saar, Betye. *Betye Saar: Extending the Table*. Roberts Projects, 2023.

Saar, Betye. "Influences | Betye Saar." *Frieze*, September 1, 2019. https://www.frieze.com/article/influences-betye-saar.

Saar, Betye. *Studio Tour with Betye Saar*. Uploaded May 3, 2016, by Los Angeles Times, YouTube, 1 min., 52 sec., https://www.youtube.com/watch?v=4jTZQzQwT_0.

Saar-Cavanaugh, Tracye. "A Family Business." In *Family Legacies: The Art of Betye, Lezley, and Alison Saar*, edited by Jessica Dallow and Barbara C. Matilsky. Ackland Art Museum, University of North Carolina at Chapel Hill / University of Washington Press, 2005.

Thomas, Sheree Renée. "Dangerous Muses: Black Women Writers Creating at the Forefront of Afrofuturism." *Literary Afrofuturism in the Twenty-First Century*, edited by Isiah Lavender III and Lisa Yaszek. Ohio State University Press, 2020, 29–38.

Thompson, Robert Farris. *Flash of the Spirit: African and Afro-American Art and Philosophy*. Vintage Books, 1983.

Turman, Aiesha. "An Afrofuturist Africana Womanist Affair." Review of *The Sexy Part of the Bible*, by Kola Boof. *Penumbra*, no. 2 (Spring 2015): 116–20.

Walker, Alice. *In Search of Our Mothers' Gardens: Womanist Prose*. Harcourt Brace Jovanovich, 1983.

Young-Scaggs, Sakena. "Afrofuturism and Womanist Phenomenology as Resistance, Resilience, and Black Joy!" *Review & Expositor* 118, no. 3 (August 2021): 332–42.

Titanium Auroras

The hard hat isn't just protection
it's a lens
a prism
catching the glare of manufactured suns
bending it

Into titanium auroras
shimmering
in the psychic stratosphere
visible only
to those who know
where to look

If you know
you know

We are chrononauts demolition mystics
boots heavy with the stardust
of undone centuries
navigating the slipstream
where cause hasn't yet met effect

Our tools resonate

tuning forks   striking
the resonant frequency   of   freedom
disrupting   the feedback loop
of systemic dystopias   inherited   despair

We are the light workers   yes
but our light   is shaped on Ikenga's altar
is forged by Ogun   in   pressure
tempered   in   defiance
It doesn't soothe   it   scours
burnishes   the possible   bright   again

We leave   not footsteps
but   contrails   of   change
shifting the atmospheric   pressure
until   breathing   itself
becomes   an   act   of   resistance
reclaiming   inner space

a persistent   dawn of new suns
engineered from the future
by   us

"Dangerous Musing"

Nisi Shawl Interviews Sheree Renée Thomas

How hard or easy is it to write poetry? How quickly does it happen?
Writing poetry is a demanding art, a negotiation between inspiration and rigorous craft. It rarely feels "easy." Sometimes, a poem arrives as a complete vision, a sudden, startling gift unwrapped in a single, exhilarating breath. These are moments of pure grace, where the poem seems to pour through me, fully formed. The lines, the imagery, the very emotional core, present themselves with a startling clarity, as if they've always existed, simply waiting for me to transcribe them. This often happens with the more visceral, emotionally charged pieces.

Other times, however, poetry is a kind of patient excavation, a meticulous, dreaming, unearthing of truth, word by deliberate word. It's like working deeply in rich soil, carefully brushing away layers to reveal an intricate root, a process demanding sustained presence and a certain kind of stubborn faith. I might spend weeks, even months, with a single line or a compelling image, allowing it to ripen and deepen before its companion lines arrive and its true form reveals itself. You must let your work rest and get "cold," so that you can create some distance from it, returning with fresh, new eyes.

This approach also influences my short fiction, like the layering of ancestral memory and cultural critique in a work like "The Grassdreaming Tree" or the gradual unfolding of spiritual traditions in "Barefoot and Midnight," where every detail builds the world and reveals a kind of hidden power.

There's no single tempo to poetry's creation; it's as varied as the human heart, but always, it's about being present, listening deeply to the unseen currents that flow beneath the surface of everyday life.

What's at the intersection of poetry and activism?

Poetry and activism intersect on rich, fertile ground where language transforms into a living, breathing force for change. Poetry, by its very nature, demands our attention, invites introspection, and possesses an ability to ignite empathy. It's a space where the personal often transcends into the political, allowing voices that have been historically silenced or on the margins to rise like sacred smoke, calling for justice, truth, and liberation.

In my own poetic practice, I find that activism is inherent in the act of giving voice to untold stories and challenging dominant narratives. For instance, my poem "Renisha McBride" directly confronts the brutal reality of violence against Black women and girls, utilizing the myth of Medusa to amplify its call for acknowledgment and justice. This violence within and beyond the community often rears its ugly head in childhood, so that many Black women and girls are navigating adolescence and/or young adulthood having survived sexual trauma and constant, pervasive attacks, societal, personal, and political against their self-esteem. After all, whole laws such as the Tignon Laws enacted in 1786 in Spanish Louisiana were legislated to criminalize the natural beauty that God gave us. Out of pure envy, Black women, free or enslaved, were forced to cover their hair with a tignon, a head-wrap, as a visible marker of their racial status, intended to diminish their perceived social standing and ward off wandering eyes of white men. Who else must contend with such weaponized, legalized disrespect? For me these poems are not merely observations. They are, in my intention, incantations and spells woven to disrupt, to heal, to activate.

This power to evoke, to make one *feel* the weight of history and the urgency of the present, is where poetry becomes an indispensable tool for activism, urging us to recognize our shared humanity and to act with courage and compassion.

How do you know when a poem or story is done?
A poem or story is done when it hums with its own complete life, every word essential, and its surrounding silence speaks as loudly as its lines. It's not a final period, but a sustained breath that settles deep within the reader. For a poem, this means that every image pulses with its intended energy, every line break serves a deliberate purpose, and the emotional arc feels resolved, even if that resolution is a lingering question or a sense of awe. Consider my poem, "The Lwa's Whisper," which concludes with "Mysteries I must embrace / Or be consumed by their silence." My hope is that it is a kind of quiet power that leaves the reader with a sense of continuous unfolding rather than rigid closure.

For my short stories, especially those with intricate plots or layered symbolism like "Aunt Dissy's Policy Dream Book," where Cassie's dreams leave indelible marks and the house itself becomes a sentient presence, I know a piece is complete when the internal logic of the world I've created feels self-contained. The characters have revealed what they needed to reveal, their journeys have reached a significant turning point, and the major implicit questions posed have found their echo. Similarly, the stories within my collection *Nine Bar Blues*, infused with the rhythms of a historic music city like Memphis, reach a point where the music of the story, even in its unresolved chords, feels deeply satisfying, as if the last note has vibrated into silence.

It's a felt sense, a knowing in the bones, a quiet sense that the spirit of the piece has found its most authentic form and has nothing more to say for now. At least not to me . . . But then again, these things are cyclical, and we bring different parts of ourselves to our reading—and our writing. I recall reading Morrison's *Jazz* multiple times. The first time I didn't think the novel had nothing to do with jazz at all and I was puzzled. The next time I returned to the novel, I was older and had seen some things! Oh, the jazz was ringing off the pages at that point. I could *see* it AND *feel* it.

It's a moment of surrender, trusting that the work will now go out into the world and find its own meaning in the hearts and minds of readers. The feeling is less about absolute perfection and more about arriving at a point where adding or subtracting would diminish its essential truth, where the notes improvising survival find their final "Strange Brutal Grace" (see page 16). It's when the cosmic choreography has completed its molecular dance and the story breathes on its own.

Several of your poems deal with Greek mythology—specifically with Cassandra and Medusa. What draws you toward these subjects? Are you familiar with Jenn Brissett's novel Elysium *(she's another Black woman writing SF and touching on "classical" myths)?*
My use of Greek mythology, particularly Cassandra and Medusa, stems from their stark parallels with Black women's and girls' experiences.

Cassandra, fated to utter truths never heeded, mirrors the historical dismissal of Black women's voices and wisdom. I am looking hard at the 2024 presidential election. Black women have been dealing with hypocrites, violent, sociopathic oppressors, and faux allies for centuries on these shores. People have been climbing on our backs to cross bridges we created for a long time in America. We know some bull when we see and hear it. The anguish of being clairvoyant but constantly unheard, of having vital insights tragically ignored until it is too late, is a familiar lament.

"Renisha McBride" directly channels the Medusa myth to pierce this veil, asking, "What kind of fear / flings open / a closed, locked door / and blasts the head off / a lone black woman?" This piece strives to demand acknowledgment of a brutal truth, pushing past comfortable silences.

Medusa, monstrously transformed after enduring violation, embodies the fierce, often demonized power of Black women's self-protection and the demonization of their natural beauty and dignity. Her gaze, capable of turning men to stone, offers a chilling metaphor for the unblinking impact of Black women's truth when it is finally, undeniably beheld. "Gorgon Root" digs deeply into this, questioning whether her "locs / that writhed and swung free / with their own breath" were perceived as a wild beauty, then transformed into a threat. These figures allow me to excavate layers of silencing, agency, and reclamation within a framework that feels both timeless and urgently current.

My short stories also navigate these mythological echoes. For instance, the transformative power and difficult choices faced by women in tales like "The Dragon Can't Dance" resonate with these ancient archetypes, exploring their journeys toward self-definition amidst chaotic forces.

I am a fan of Jenn Brissett's *Elysium*. Her work shines as a great approach to classical myths through a Black diasporic lens, and is, in my estimation, groundbreaking. Her reimagining expands the very firmament of our understanding, revealing how these foundational stories can be recontextualized to speak to fresh truths about identity and enduring history.

Per Percy Shelley, poets are "the unacknowledged legislators of the world." Your poems are powerful, your prose is poetic. What would you like to be your first planetwide law?
If I could pass one planetwide law, it would be this: Every being shall be taught, from their earliest breath, the profound practice of radical empathy, understanding that another's pain is a tremor in our shared humanity, and another's joy, a light for us all. This law, deeply rooted in the philosophy that underpins much of my work, aims to cultivate a fundamental shift in how we relate to each other and the world, recognizing that our destinies are interwoven. It calls for actively seeking to understand, to feel, and to respond to the experiences of others, fostering a world where compassion is the most powerful force. If humanity as a species has shared empathy, the real kind, not that performative and when-it's-convenient version, then we spend less time fighting over resources and more time solving other pressing problems on the planet. In fact, some of those problems might soon become obsolete, since we'd be more from a place of shared empathy, shared destinies, and not profits and power over people and the other vital life forces on our planet.

You sometimes mention members of the Yoruba pantheon in your stories—Elegba, for example, in "Child's Play." Are you, like me, a practitioner of Yoruba religious traditions?
The Yoruba pantheon, including figures like Elegba, represents for me an ancestral cosmology that acknowledges the profound interconnectedness of all things—nature, humanity, and the divine. While I may not define myself as a "practitioner" in a formal, initiated sense, I engage with the orisha as archetypal energies, powerful forces of nature, and profound guides in my life and my creative work. They embody principles and wisdoms that resonate deeply with my understanding of the world and the Black

experience, offering a framework for navigating life's crossroads and challenges.

This spiritual connection extends deeply into the practice of Hoodoo, a powerful African-American spiritual tradition that is a vital branch from the great ancestral tree of spiritual practices rooted in the Congo, Benin, Nigeria, Sierra Leone, and other parts of Africa. It is a lineage woven into my own family's history, a system of folk wisdom focused on practical results, protection, healing, and influencing everyday life through natural elements and ancestral wisdom, ancestral veneration. For instance, the Bakongo/Kikongo cosmogram forms the root of a similar, potent symbol found in Hoodoo, a testament to this unbroken line of knowledge we carried with us from Africa to many shores. This cosmogram, representing the cycle of life, death, and rebirth, also echoes symbolic structures found in Kemetic Medu Neter, the hieroglyphs often understood as "divine words." In my poetry, such as "The Lwa's Whisper," Papa Legba subtly guides at "*my mind's crossroads*," and Ogun's fire "*flickers restless in my hands / Ready to build or break*."

In my work, Hoodoo appears not as an outdated caricature, but as a living current of knowledge and power shared across generations, often tied to the land and the endurance of Black people. It is a form of spiritual technology that also uses technology, that "mojotech" as evoked by the artist Betye Saar. For example, "Jigganaut" speaks to teachings about "root dance" and "spirit dance," linking movement and rhythm to profound spiritual knowledge. I wrote "Child's Play" inspired after some of my own teaching experiences and not long after writer and former student Daniel José Older had completed his spiritual initiation. He was still an EMT in New York City at the time, and for me, his healing work was hand in hand with the other good he did in the community. He was a good resource for my questions when writing that story. Also, my first home in Harlem was on Strivers' Row in a beautiful brownstone owned by a wonderful Yoruba priestess whose crown was Sango, while my adoptive NYC family, those who welcomed me and showed me the city's wonders, were Haitian. I had a lot of important crossroads with these spiritual traditions that helped shape my witnessing, exploration, and personal practices and allowed me to see firsthand how deeply connected the diaspora roads are.

For me, this spirituality isn't a rigid doctrine, but a fluid, living connection to the mystical and the ancestral traditions that inform my writing voice. It's a knowing that transcends the purely rational, embracing the marvelous real inherent in the Black experience.

Characters and situations appear and reappear in your stories and poems—is there a Sheree Renéeniverse populated by playful gold cherubim and gorgeous Black Gorgons rocking telepathic dreadlocks? And is there something like a timeline, a secret history of your imaginings?
Yes, my imaginative landscape pulses with its own intricate life in interconnected worlds. This is a layered storycloth woven from folklore, myth, personal memory, and the rich currents of Black experience, possessing less a rigid chronology and more a secret history I draw upon at will. I am actively exploring more of these specific worlds in longer forms, including novelettes, novellas, and future works, where certain characters and locales deepen their shared existence. The three sisters from "Head Static," "Shanequa's Blues, or, Another Shotgun Lullaby" (*Nine Bar Blues*), "Love Hangover" (*Trouble the Waters*), and "Shoop-B-Doop & Cop'Em" (*Ring Shout on Saturn*) exist in a world that connects to other stories. The choreography in the story "The Dragon Can't Dance" reappears in *Mojorhythm*, in "See Me! Look Me!" when the heroine's friends attempt to rescue her from the pop star Isis's clutches, and readers

learn that there is an important connection between the music mogul that runs Isis's label in "The Beautifulest" and "Can't Stop, Don't Stop." The recurring dream imagery and ancestral presences found in tales like "Aunt Dissy's Policy Dream Book" or the other connections to music and the South in *Nine Bar Blues* all blend into this interconnected reality. In my poetry such as "Gorgon Root," the motifs of the rooted, the unyielding, and the transformative suggest a continuous, evolving exploration of core themes across this shared realm. They sort of hint at an underlying design that binds this particular universe where every narrative and verse adds another layer, inviting readers to discover its hidden connections and echoes.

You refer to the Maafa in many of your pieces. What does that word mean, and why do you prefer it to other terms for what you're talking about?

Maafa is a Swahili term meaning "great tragedy," "great disaster," or "great suffering." It encompasses the profound devastation of the Middle Passage, the Transatlantic slave trade, the Middle Journey across the Atlantic Ocean. Historical accounts indicate that approximately 15 percent of kidnapped Africans—nearly two million people—died during this brutal crossing, their bodies tossed overboard, with some voyages seeing mortality rates as high as 33 percent. This immense forced migration is why the largest populations of Africans outside the continent of Africa now reside in Brazil, the United States, and Haiti.

I prefer "Maafa" as it acknowledges the full spiritual, cultural, and psychological catastrophe visited upon African peoples and their descendants. It is crucial to use proper terminology for cultural and historical events, and Maafa accurately reflects this immense, ongoing suffering. Its origins are rooted in African linguistic traditions, chosen by scholars and activists to reclaim the narrative and honor the depth of this historical wound.

You've written and edited prose and poetry, and you've written comic books too (including "The World Is Not Ready" featuring Storm and Black Panther in Marvel's Voices: Legends #1 *and a novel,* Black Panther: Panther's Rage*). Have you written play scripts? Film or television scripts? Songs? Which forms of creativity are you most interested in engaging with?*

My creative journey spans diverse artistic landscapes, from prose and poetry to comics. Writing comics like Marvel's "The World Is Not Ready," demands prose economy, while adapting a graphic novel into a traditional novel, as with *Black Panther: Panther's Rage*, challenges me to expand interiority and translate visual dynamism into lyrical narrative. I also explored new frontiers in game writing as a narrative consultant and futurist for Mercedes-Benz's collaboration with Sony PlayStation's *Dreams: Imagine Futures.*

Though I haven't penned a full stage play (I have some one-acts), I think my prose often carries the orality and musicality foundational to dramatic works. I have written a screenplay, *Haint Blue*, and find writing fantasy and horror, the magical stuff, for the screen deeply intriguing. It's a great time to be doing so, especially with the successes of projects like Jordan Peele's groundbreaking movies and Ryan Coogler's recent *Sinners*, which I really enjoyed, particularly for its respectful depiction of Hoodoo and its celebration of Black American musical genius. My exploration of songwriting also acknowledges language's inherent musicality, a theme woven through *Nine Bar Blues.*

What do you look for when you edit an anthology? Is there a certain plot structure, a certain voice you want in a story you decide to include? Do you decide which authors you want ahead of time?

Editing an anthology is like alchemy. You are seeking a universal treasure with disparate elements you hope to transform into a cohesive yet diverse collection. I seek stories possessing undeniable voice, those that transport me instantly into their unique rhythm and emotional landscape. While plot structure is important, it's often the visceral feeling, emotional truth, and sheer imaginative audacity that truly captivate. My inclination is toward character-driven narratives, where inner lives linger long after the final page.

I typically do not preselect authors, although I do sometimes have writers in mind who I think would create something special and cool. I usually have open submissions as well to allow fitting voices for the theme to emerge organically. After all, if you only invite those you already know, how will you find the truly new and innovative voices? I seek the unexpected, the boundary-pushing, and the deeply human—tales that evoke wonder and leave a lasting impression. My goal is always to create a collection celebrating both established and emerging talents, enriching the speculative fiction landscape and honoring different kinds of storytelling.

You've shared a passionate essay about some very particular pieces of art in this book; it's poetic and moving, demanding and lush. Midway through, you quote bell hooks's Art on My Mind: Visual Politics. *What is your "art on the walls," the beauty that gives you the powerfully transformative tools you write with?*

My "art on the walls" is a manifold, ever-evolving tapestry. First, there are the ancestral stories whispered down through generations, the vibrant oral traditions of my Memphis upbringing where grandparents and their friends were masterful storytellers. This oral tradition constantly shapes my poetry's rhythms and its ability to conjure worlds. My art also includes the rich hues of Black culture and the raw beauty of the natural world, particularly the profound presence of the Mississippi River. It's the collected wisdom of literary forebears like Henry Dumas, Octavia E. Butler, Toni Cade Bambara, Arthur Flowers, Gayl Jones, Audre Lorde, Alice Walker, Toni Morrison, Ray Bradbury, Edgar Allan Poe, and

Zora Neale Hurston, whose words are living maps to liberation and understanding. Their narratives, exploring the extraordinary within the ordinary, deeply resonate with themes in my short fiction. My poetry directly engages this "art on the walls": "Rafters Hold" speaks of a structure holding memory and lineage and is inspired by Toni Morrison's *Beloved*. Visual arts help me link the language of dreams and history to transformative magic, an innovative written flesh.

Conversely, what about some of the white-supremacist pieces of public art you've been forced to encounter?
Exposure to white-supremacist public art, like the statue of Nathan Bedford Forrest, especially for children, is a jarring encounter, a visible reminder of a brutal past that dehumanizes and minimizes the horrors visited upon your ancestors for global profit. It's especially galling when you know some of these monuments, like the Forrest one that once was in Memphis, were built long after the Confederacy lost the Civil War, but placed at a time when Black citizens were exerting their civil rights to vote and not to be financially exploited by paying taxes for services you were denied based on racial apartheid. Paradoxically, I derive from it a sharper clarity on the enduring struggle and a fiery resolve to craft counter-narratives that affirm Black resilience, beauty, and humanity. Such monuments fuel my commitment to use words as acts of defiance, healing, and reimagining, transforming historical wounds into catalysts for a more urgent song. This is mirrored in my poetry, which seeks to dismantle imaginings built on lies and leave open fertile ground, and in my fiction.

My award-winning novelette, "Madame & the Map: A Journey in Five Movements," and "Sweet Chariots in Dixieland," which I wrote in 1999 at Clarion West, were conceived years before the Take 'Em Down 901 movement successfully removed the Forrest monument from its prominent placement in UT Memphis's park in the Medical District. These narratives explore the complex, enduring presence of such historical figures and their symbols, examining how they haunt the landscape and the collective memory. My stories assert new truths in spaces once claimed by oppressive histories, exploring how acts of artistic or communal reclamation can confront and transmute their power.

When teaching "Dialogue and Dialect" classes, I frequently refer to your remarks on code-switching. Please say some more smart things about the choices people make when they speak in different ways to different people about different things.

Code-switching, for many, is an artful, necessary act of navigation, a testament to linguistic dexterity and cultural intelligence. We fluidly adapt our language, cadence, and vocabulary not to deny self, but to communicate across diverse spaces, a sophisticated dance of identity. This is particularly true in Southern Black communities, where repetition, for instance, often signals emphasis, not redundancy. When writers translate speech to the page, these choices become powerful acts. Rendering dialect can be profound cultural affirmation, inviting readers to truly *hear* a character's world, honoring diverse linguistic forms. Conversely, standardizing speech can erase identity and nuance. A writer's choice in capturing specific rhythms or slang is not merely about authenticity. It speaks to power, representation, and the nuanced portrayal of human experience. It's about letting our language sing with its true, complex voice, its authentic mother tongues.

You've said your mother read science fiction, and that your grandfather sometimes told "scary stories." What do you remember about your mother's early influence on your taste for speculative fiction? And what can you tell us about the scariness in your grandfather's stories—what were they about?

My mother's early influence on my taste for speculative fiction was foundational, like the feeder roots of a pecan tree. She loves science fiction and has a great imagination, and was a visual artist, often drawing and sculpting when I was small. Through her I discovered stories could be portals, questioning reality and expanding my understanding of our world. I read authors like Poe, Bradbury, King, and Straub because she read them, along with Tolkien, Jackie Collins, *fun times*, and *Omni Magazine*. She also introduced me to Black Arts Movement authors like Ishmael Reed, Sonia Sanchez, and Larry Neal, and a ton of nonfiction.

My grandfather's scary stories blended haint tales, terrifying real-life accounts of how he and others were treated during America's racial apartheid era—euphemistically called "Jim Crow"—and his own vivid biblical retellings. These narratives taught me a reverence for storytelling, an appreciation for the unseen and the thin veil between worlds. His storytelling thrived in the liminal spaces of what was taught and what was lived. He rooted me deeply in rich, unsettling folklore and real history, not the whitewashed mess of fantasies they try to feed us, shaping the subtle psychological horror I evoke. The most potent fear, I learned, often comes from what you don't quite see, or what you almost see. And from what is unsaid.

Someone told me you once met Michael Jackson at a science fiction bookstore. What was that like?

That was a surreal and unforgettable moment, a quiet convergence of two seemingly disparate worlds. I met Michael while working at Forbidden Planet and also editing at Random House, an epic experience laced with a little cloak-and-dagger secrecy. This was back when Forbidden Planet was directly across from the Strand

and when that mysterious Black diaspora book archive/store was above us on an upper floor in the same building. The owner later auctioned his amazing collection off to one of the local universities, but it was book heaven while it lasted. Our bookstore manager, of course, didn't tell us who was coming in advance, only that we weren't allowed to wild out, and to give them whatever they wanted on their running tab.

First, a limo pulled up, then two bodyguards stormed in, dressed like Terry Lewis and Jimmy Jam. Children with bandanas followed, making me think it was perhaps a special visit from the Make-A-Wish Foundation. But then, when Michael himself strolled in wearing his fedora, a black mask, and that iconic glove, I liked ta fell out. My manager, may he rest in peace, pressed a calming but firm hand on my shoulder, and I managed to pull myself together, surprised by my own latent fan reaction. Embarrassed to say but I was about to cut up like those teens in the old Elvis and MJ footage. For real! But I glanced around to note how patrons were handling it—one guy in a Superman cape merely looked over, then returned to thumbing through the erotic comics, all nonchalant, or performing nonchalance like I was. Michael was tall, had a deep voice full of full-grown bass, and asked for Magic cards. I was thrilled! Couldn't tell me nothing for weeks.

You're currently the editor of the venerable Magazine of Fantasy & Science Fiction. *What's it like taking over a seventy-five-year-old institution like that? Are you ever surprised to find yourself sitting in the editor's chair there? What's your biggest wish for the publication?* Being editor of *The Magazine of Fantasy & Science Fiction* feels like stepping into a storied river—an immense honor and responsibility, especially since I also read it as a child. My greatest wish is for it to remain a vibrant, inclusive home for thought-provoking speculative fiction. I want it to be a space where emerging voices find their footing alongside established masters, continually expanding the very boundaries of our genre. During my tenure, I want to strengthen its infrastructural support, bring it up to the twenty-first century in terms of its online presence, build more community for its authors and readers, and deepen its commitment to ensuring our pages reflect the beautiful, complex storytelling power of our world. It's about nurturing discovery and surprise in every issue, always reminding readers that the fantastic abounds, and its myriad stories are for all.

I was at Eileen Gunn's a few days ago and she showed me her copy of Scarab*—so superbly gorgeous! Now I need to know more about it. So . . . what was it? When do we get more?*
Oh! Yes, Eileen was so kind as to buy a copy and she told me I was selling them too low, lol. *Scarab* was a limited-edition, handmade, Coptic-bound art book, an anthology of original speculative fiction and poetry. Ama Patterson, Tony Medina, Andrea Hairston, Pan Morigan, Liz Roberts, and a lot of other authors. It was printed by an employee-owned co-op, and some sections were printed on handmade paper. Recently, Andrea and Pan and I have been talking about possibly reprinting it, or maybe creating a second volume.

What's a question you wish I had asked you? What's your answer to it?
A question I wish you had asked: "Beyond the challenges and insights, what brings you the most joy in your creative life?"

My answer: The deepest joy in my creative life springs from connection. It's the moment a reader shares how a story or poem impacted them, making them feel truly seen. It's the marvel of witnessing another writer's brilliance ignite on the page, or the collaborative dance of bringing an anthology to life. Sometimes writers are a hot mess of ego, arrogance, and insecurity, but for the most part, they are kind, insightful, remarkable beings who bring a lot of value to our lives, mine included. Storytellers brought a lot of comfort to my childhood and opened a powerful window to the world.

It is the boundless freedom of imagination, knowing that within the realm of story, anything is possible—that dreams can leave indelible marks, or conversations with ancestors can unfold across centuries—that makes working in words worthwhile. Knowing that words, deeply imagined, lovingly crafted, and generously shared, can forge bridges, mend wounds, and illuminate pathways forward, creating wonder and shared humanity across geographies, cultures, and time. Not a bad way to spend some of your day, thank you!

Ring Shout on Saturn

No dirt floor warm
beneath bare shuffling feet
this time
only the deck plate humming
low static cold
through worn boot soles
this magnetic dust perhaps
from Saturn's halo
billion billion ice motes whispering
forget   remember   forget
in the void's vast cathedral throat

No pine grove circle
no moss-draped oak stands witness here
just the Ship's curved spine
bending back on itself always
and the rings immense indifferent
glittering like god's discarded calculations
fractured mathematics flung hard
across the black

We make the circle anyway
counter-clockwise turn

against Ship's regulated spin
against the drift toward silence, erasure
remembering rhythms our people made
bent low, adapting, surviving
blood-laws meant to break the spirit whole
on Georgia coast Carolina fields deep deep
in the Tennessee Mississippi Delta mud swamp heat

Now translated here light years gone
the muscle memory finds us
Hands clap sharp, make thunder where there is no air
feet stomp, shuffle, slide, raise ghost dust
from pressed composite floor
one voice calls raw, cuts deep
through regulated silence clean
another answers, echoes, multiplies
          defiant blooms
Ancestor hear us now Olokun Yemaya Legba
hear us still
across this killing distance
this cold unpromised terrible space

They try to outlaw the drum
the dance, the tongue
call our histories contraband
our unbound futures forbidden data
try to lock down memory
erase it in smooth efficient servers
archive delete chain the holy ghost
rattling wild inside the Ship's machine heart
but the body remembers always

The Shout builds electric
a current jumping spine to spine
calloused hand to calloused hand
ecstasy a fierce unexpected bloom
against low-g nausea the head's slow spin vertigo
spirit possession shaking this fabricated hull down
to its tired loosening rivets
finding god finding us finding home making home
here
not on that red dust ball orbiting below
not on lost blue Earth that green forgotten memory
but here now in the sacred turn
the testifying released breath
the unbroken circle

Stomping freedom's fierce vibration
deep onto the cold dust settling heavy now
from Saturn's borrowed indifferent light
a ring shout defiant ecstatic necessary
claiming this single sliver of hull
this hard moment, this thin air
making this patch of Ship floor finally
holy ground.

Thirteen Year Long Song

"If I could have another life, I'd take it," he said, sitting upright in the straight back chair. "This one ain't worth ten cents to me. I'd like to do things for myself again. Would give everything I've got for that."

He was sitting on his porch, staring at a field so green, it almost hurt his eyes. Rachel, Doc's middle daughter, had cut the grass for him again, and this time, she hadn't bagged it yet. The grass lay in soft piles and clumps all along the neatly trimmed rows. Suddenly, he wanted to jump again, to leap and roll in the mounds of grass like he did when he was little. If he could, he would scoot the red, peeling chair back against the leaning house's wall. If he could, he would leap clean over the front steps, scattering the piles like great clouds of green dust.

He sat there and remembered when his back was both iron and water, when his legs pumped like two pistons, and his feet flowed like the river beyond his acres; when his whole body carried him whenever and wherever he wanted to go. If he could, he would leap across the fence, which separated his land from the company's, and give those Viscerol folks a rough piece of his mind. Back in the day, he'd done more for less. But the world he lived in now didn't look like anything Doc recognized. Seemed like people had given up, even the earth itself. He gazed at his little patch of land and remembered how lush it had all been.

Pollen got in his eyes, and the orbs, one brown and one blue, soon covered in mist.

Outside, the wind picked up a loose clump of grass, along with his wishes, and spun the green stalks into the air. A lazy S, the bottoms of the stalks waved like flags in the sky above him. He sat there in the chair, one hand balled into a tight fist, the other's nails dug into the rotten wood. Memory poured down on him like hard rain. Behind a curtain of pines and cypresses, a pair of eyes watched, and something listened.

A few days later, Doc rose, feeling more tired than he ever had. More tired than all those years ago when the nurses had stuck him so full of needles that he thought he'd turned into a pin cushion. "Y'all done drew so much blood, now you gon' have to give some back," he'd said, but the men had only smiled. Whatever they knew then, they didn't speak, and what they told him later he wished it was a lie.

Now Doc's whole body felt like he fell down the stairs and hit every step on the way down. He kept waking in the middle of the night with soil all over the thin white sheets and clumps of dirt all up in his hair. Doc didn't know what he had done or where he had gone. He took the dirty sheets and held them like dark secrets, balled them up like fists, and hid them under his bed. He tried to bathe, but he couldn't get himself in the lukewarm water before Rachel arrived. He could hear her fussing at the front door. His whole body flushed with embarrassment.

"Doc? Oh, Doc!" she cried and tossed the keys into the amber dish on the old phone stand. "Where are you?"

On Rachel's best day, her whisper was more of a shout.

Doc fumbled with his pants so long, he tired himself out, had to sit on the toilet seat just to catch his breath. He grabbed a yellow Bourbon & Bacon T-shirt and pulled it over his head. His beard got caught in the neck. Doc untangled it with his fingers, then stroked the white strands straight and smooth until the ends curled into cottony wisps.

"There's something in the blood," he muttered. Doc had known for over a dozen years that something more than memory coursed through his veins. His body was full of poison. They all were. Those with good sense had already gone and got out.

"Doc, you hear me?"

He took a deep breath before Rachel could come around the corner, bustling with those big hands that didn't know nothing about being ginger. He heard her hand jangling the knob at the door.

"Girl, why you always tryna bust in on me?" he asked. "You know this doxin got me moving slow."

"Dioxin, Doc," Rachel said and laughed. "And ain't nobody trying to see nothing you got!" She put her bike helmet away and fluffed her flattened hair.

He opened the door and waved away her helping hand. "I got more than plenty."

"Come on out of here, Daddy," she said, and chuckled, opening the window. "It's stuffy in here and too hot today to be fussing. I done cooked this food and I need you to eat it," she said, side-eying his linen-less bed, "so I can get on back to work."

"Y'all still protesting?"

Rachel sighed, forehead nothing but a crease. "Some of them still out there. Not as many as before."

"Ain't gon' do no good," Doc said. "You can't shame the shameless."

"Well, I don't know one way or the other," she said and bit off a hangnail. "It is good to know somebody still trying . . ."

"Even if these muthafuckas ain't listening?"

"Daddy!" Rachel said. "Don't start up again. Last time you made a ruckus, your pressure went up."

"My pressure didn't go up, my patience just low!"

"Exactly! And either way, we got to get these coins, so . . ."

Doc stiffened, lowered his voice. "I ain't mad at you, baby girl. You do what you can. And I appreciate it. I'm just saying . . ."

"I know, Daddy. I know."

Doc stared out the window, frowning at the silhouette that overshadowed his land. He raised a clenched fist up and covered the water tower with his knuckles.

"Did you crank the truck?"

"Not yet," she said, and watched him lower his bony arm to tie his robe around his waist.

"When you gon' do it?" he asked. "When I finally get ready to go, I want to be able to get on down. Big Daddy can't crank hisself."

"Soon, Doc; you act like I'm getting my nails done here. Let me clean up this kitchen after you eat, and then I'll start up Big Daddy. You and I both know that ole truck is just fine. Big Daddy gon' outlast both of us. Besides, you been up and about, I see. But you looking frail. Don't you want something to eat? Don't look like you ate all day."

Doc scratched his beard, avoided her eyes. "Not hungry."

"Doc, you got to eat. Can't be sitting up in here, nibbling on leaves, and that jug of water still half full." She clapped her hands, brass bracelets singing like wind chimes. "I'm going to fix you something extra, for later tonight. Put some meat on them bones," she said, and headed for the kitchen.

"Ain't nothing wrong with my bones," Doc whispered, muttering under his breath. "Ground is wrong." He mourned his garden and his empty fields, soured burial ground of what used to be. His last crops had come out so scraggly, he finally gave it up. Yield so bad, neither a weevil nor a worm would want it.

Anyone that knew him knew his family's roots had run deep in that land. Now he and Rachel and that rust heap he called a truck was all that was left. Outside, the wind whispered and sounded like somebody was calling his name. He wrapped the robe tighter around his waist and peered through the window. Nothing but shadows and wind. And that poison plant's tower.

He glanced over his shoulder and remembered the muddied linen he had hidden. No need to worry Rachel. Besides, he had no idea where he had been.

When Rachel came in with that smile of hers, the smile that never quite covered the worry in her eyes, he decided he would go ahead and eat whatever she had taken the time to make. No sense adding his worries to hers. The girl had enough.

"This is good," Doc said, licking his fingertip. "I don't think I could eat a mite more."

Rachel took the tray of pancakes from him and frowned. "You ain't ate nothing but syrup!"

Doc shrugged and drew the sheet around his shoulders. He couldn't seem to get warm. "I'm sorry, Slick Bean. Ain't had much appetite. Them hotcakes are good, but whatever I eat these days feels funny in my throat."

Rachel grunted. "Funny, huh?" She shook her head and eyed the empty Aunt Jemima bottle, as if she might answer back. "You ain't getting a fever, are you?"

Doc waved Rachel away. "Go on, girl. Don't want you to be late." He lay his head on the flattened pillow and closed his eyes, whispered all night in his sleep.

The radio coughed and sputtered. ". . . administration dismisses EPA scientists . . . Toxic Substances Control Act of 1976 gutted . . ." Doc reached up and turned the channel. "There's an old flame, burning in your eyes . . . that tears can't drown, and makeup can't disguise . . ." Alabama and a chorus of cicadas filled the front yard with song. Doc turned, confused. He climbed out of his bed, big toe searching for his house shoes.

He stood up. The wave of sound droned around him, the rhythm filling his head and clouding his eyes. The food Rachel had prepared him was resting on a plate on his nightstand. The window he swore he had closed was wide open, gaping like a dark mouth.

The hair on his arms rippled, and he caught himself from crying out. He hadn't been afraid for so long, he had forgotten how fear might feel. Rachel kept one of those drugstore cell phones for him, but he rarely used it because there was no one left to call. He thought about picking it up and calling Rachel, but he wasn't so sure what he would say once she answered. *Hey, daughter, a haint chasing me all through my sleep. Hey, daughter, I got mud on my clothes and mud all cross the bottom of my feet.* Rachel wouldn't understand none of that. And she had already started to watching him out of the corner of her eyes, when she thought he didn't notice. He knew what his most loyal child had been searching for, and he was determined to hold back the fatigue that kept calling him to linger longer in his sleep. Whatever was chasing him would have to come harder than that.

When Doc put on his knock-around boots and stepped out into the yard to greet the day, he liked to fell down when he saw the ruckus in his yard. A big-ass crack, zigzagging long like Moses in the mountain high, had separated what was left of his family's property. "Sweet geegee, great day in the morning," he said, and stumbled down the porch steps so fast, he nearly flipped over. He had never, in all the long minutes and hours of his days, seen a sight like this.

The yard was all torn apart, as if a great hand from above had reached down and unzipped the dark earth. He walked over to the crack nearest him and eased over, his knee and his whole leg tense. Doc craned his head to see how far the hole went, and realized there was no bottom to see, just darkness leading down and thick, twisted roots and stones and things he wasn't sure he actually did see.

What he did recognize was the same source of all his and the town's troubles, that red-stained poison that the Viscerol plant had cursed them with. At one point, everyone and their mama had worked at Viscerol, and the money was good, too. But one by one, family by family, a sickness had come down on each of them, until finally, the only healthy families left had packed up their things and got on down the road. Only a few stubborn, hard scrabblers stayed on, Rachel included. That bloody water ran through each dark vein across the town, until only a few families remained. Rachel was all of Doc's own, the others, he knew, long gone, perhaps to sweeter grounds. Silver citadels of columns and pipes, smokestacks and tanks rose along the town's skyline like rusted spikes. "Relocate Fair Property Buy-Out" signs dotted abandoned lawns, jagged yellow teeth. Houses, once full of light and life, sat on their haunches, full of furniture, roofs lolling like broken baby dolls, doors flung open, bloated, wooden tongues.

Scavengers came to take what the families had not deemed worthy to carry on. Whole families had disappeared, it seemed, overnight, leaving all that they once owned behind to decay in the town's deadly dust. And now Doc stood, staring down into what he thought had to be the dark face of God's judgment. The Good Lord took man and put him in the garden to work and keep it, but from what Doc could tell, man had done a piss-poor job.

And what had that hard, scrabble-back preacher said, before he, too, showed his backside to Viscerol and the town, with its labyrinth, prison-like plant that spewed poisons, and the giant water tower emblazoned with its red V? They had transgressed the laws, violated the statutes. They had broken the everlasting covenants, turned an ancient blessing into a new curse. Old Rev. Bowen had preached a word that day, as he took the church Bible and its baptismal altar with him. That they never should have let Viscerol build on their fertile land. That they should have turned those jobs down, and the money, too. Now newborns of townsfolk, who had been there for generations, were being born so sick they had to carry the future away from there.

Doc didn't know what that was, rumbling deep inside the open door of earth, but he knew he didn't want to be standing around when whatever it was came busting through. He bolted up the steps as fast as his legs would carry him and knew exactly what he must do. He planned to be long gone, before the skies rolled up like a scroll and the heavens vanished like smoke.

#

"Doc! Oh, Doc! What is all this you got piled up in the truck?" Rachel stomped up the steps, the screen door banging shut behind her. Her bike lay on the ground, the rusted kickstand jutting out like a swollen tongue. The house was dark and the whole sky, too, but she could still see that Doc had emptied half the house and had it sitting up in the back of Big Daddy.

A groan met her before she walked in his room.

"What did you say, Doc?"

She put her helmet down and found him lying on his side in his bed, staring out the window. Rachel missed the times when he was a handful, when she used to get off work and find him stumbling, mumbling in the dark, cranky as ever. Then he would cuss like a thief with an empty wallet, tell her story after story about some slight from the past, a friend who stole away from the broken, poisoned town without even saying goodbye, the neighbor who still had his good clippers and never bothered to acknowledge the debt. The other one, whose grass he cut as if it was his own, when the poison had made the man's skin peel off under the tainted bloodstained tap water. Thirteen years, he and his friends had suffered, undergoing varying stages of collapse and decay, until only Doc remained, steadfast and stubborn on his family's land. But it wasn't the land that worried her. It was his mind. Now it didn't even look like he was going to be able to hold on to that.

"Where have all the fireflies gone?"

Doc pointed a finger at the darkness outside. "There used to be clouds of them, all up through here. When y'all was little, you used to run out and try to catch them . . ."

"In jelly jars, yes," she said, "I remember, Daddy. Why are you worried about fireflies? We ain't seen them in years, now. And why have you tired yourself out, packing up this old house by yourself? I told you, when you were ready to move, I'd be ready to move with you."

"'Cuz they gone like everything else."

"I ain't gone. I'm still here."

He turned to look at her. "Yes, you are. You and that old maple in the yard, the only things softening the heat. What you gon' do when my eyes close?"

"Oh, Daddy," Rachel said and brushed some lint out of her eye. "Why you always got to say that?"

Doc didn't answer for a while. He raised up on his elbow and craned his head, as if listening to a sound far off in the darkness. The wind whistled and the little strip of curtain fluttered like a moth's wing. Finally, he turned to her, his beard jutted out like a question mark. "Because I don't want you to be the last one left here."

Rachel rubbed her palms together, the sound like sandpaper. "What I tell you? When you leave, I leave." The moon rose from behind a cloud, the light spilling over the windowsill into the room of darkness, a sign and a symbol. "We got to leave soon. The ground ain't good."

Doc laid his head down and drifted off to sleep.

The next night, Rachel could hear the sound before she pulled up. When she dropped her bike and first walked up the gravel driveway, little husks crunching under her feet, she thought the sound was coming from the tree. She stumbled on an upturned root that hadn't been there before.

"Where did you come from?" she asked, and unsnapped the chin strap of her helmet, but the tree was silent. As she walked, the driveway sounded extra gravelly, almost crunchy. She thought she was moving carefully, but she tripped again. Not a root this time, but something hard, shell-like. Rachel turned on the flashlight on her phone and peered at the biggest husk she'd ever seen, big as a lunchbox, liked to jumped right out of her skin.

"Lawd," she cried before she could catch herself, started laughing at her own fool self. Then she looked around and saw that the yard and the porch steps, all the way up to the front door, were filled with empty shells. The warm spring night chilled her, the fine hairs on her arm prickled in alarm. She was fine until the air filled with a high-pitched, shrill song. The sound was deafening. Suddenly, everything about Doc's yard seemed strange and frightening. The driveway littered with hills of hollow husks, and the maple tree's branches that hung low in the darkness, as if weighed down by a burden only the wind could see. Hundreds of them, perhaps thousands, resting and waiting in the limbs, singing that song that made all of her flesh ripple and itch. A deep, pulsing sound like a great alarm, ringing through the dark scroll of sky.

And then she saw it. A wave of movement rushing up from what looked like the biggest hole she had ever seen. A mini–Grand Canyon ripped right open in her daddy's front yard. A few more steps to the right and she would have been good and gone.

Rachel hunched her back, held her helmet like a weapon, and when a low humming buzzed her left ear, she flew up the front steps, practically barreling through the door.

"Doc!"

Inside the house, they covered the floor like a glittering, blue-green blanket. Rachel shuffled through them, trying not to cry out as they crunched beneath her feet. She found Doc lying there, wrapped up in his bedsheets, mud all over the bed, mud all over the floor. She called to him above the din, but he only turned his eyes away and would not answer. The more he refused to speak, lips sewed up, the more she found herself ripping at invisible seams. In her time, the town had seen its share of plagues, but this was a new marvel. And Doc didn't want to speak. He didn't even seem to want to be anymore. He seemed to be waiting, wrapped in his muddy cocoon, surrounded by the insects that cuddled him as if he was their own true kin. He held the sheets so fast that she grew weary and stopped wrestling with him. She patted his shoulder and left him to the mud, and the wind, and the rising moon.

Desperate for answers, she found herself breaking and entering the old public library. Shamed, Rachel asked for forgiveness as she crossed herself and climbed and picked her way through overturned piles of books, laid out like waterlogged corpses, all that remained of it. After some time, Rachel discovered a thin volume, *Cicadas: The Puzzle and the Problem.* She forced herself to slow her breathing, to focus her eyes on the handwritten text. An entomologist's entry read, *Magicicada tredecula*, but by the time Rachel got to Doc's house, all she could remember was "magic Dracula," and something about thirteen-year-long broods and spirits. From the book's maps, no broods of cicadas had ever been documented anywhere near that part of the state, but given the damage already done, no telling what else the plants had unleashed on the town and its few remaining citizens.

"They can't sting or bite," she'd read at the library, her wheels now crunching as she pulled up to Doc's house. "They sing," the book said. "Their song can be a hymn-like trance, a lullaby that lulls weaker spirits to waste away, while others rejuvenate, are resurrected."

"They don't bite, huh, but they sho'll can swarm and scare the mess out of you," she'd thought. One of the chapters mentioned something about a divine test, a path to transformation. Rachel didn't have time for none of that. "Hush, loud bugs," she said as she slammed on her brakes. "Ain't no way in hell I'm finna let some devil dust bugs suck up my daddy's soul!"

Rachel was kicking the piles of shells out of her way, determined to get Doc, when the ground shifted and rumbled beneath her. "What did I say that for!" she muttered as she held onto the porch rail.

Low clouds of cicadas swept from the holes in the grass, hovered in the sky, headed for the maple tree. Rachel ran into the house and locked the door behind her but remembered the open window in Doc's room.

"Daddy!" she cried, racing to his bedroom. "I need you to get up." She reached for him but discovered that he was covered in a sticky film. If he hadn't been her own father, scared as she was, she would have left him right there.

Rachel wiped her palms on her jacket and reached for Doc again. She unpeeled the cottony layers and tossed the dirty sheet onto the floor.

"I need you to help me, Daddy," she said. She spoke to him quiet, calm, like he did when she was a small child and had fallen and didn't want to get up. He had always been there for her; that was why she vowed she would always be there for him.

"We don't have to live in this place no more. We can leave, Daddy. You can leave. We can go right now. Come with me." She peeled the spider web–like substance from across his eyes. She was relieved to see recognition there.

"All right, Slick Bean," he said, as if waking from a dream, and reached for her outstretched hand. He held it, letting the warmth spread through his palms, and then he forced himself to rise.

They waded through the carpet of husks until they were standing outside.

"Daddy, did you see that hole in the ground? I swear, I ain't never seen nothing like this in my whole life. You think it's fracking that did all that? Brought all these damn bugs?"

"Not all. I did it," Doc said as he leaned on her, letting her guide him to the green truck door. He didn't wait for her reply. "You know how it is! Here, people don't always say what they mean or mean what they say. They just be talking, thinking aloud. But sometimes, out here, the land be listening." He turned to the wind, the piles of husks, the moon and the shadows. "Can't a person think aloud sometime? Wrassle with a thought until they come up with their own good answer?"

He stood and pointed at the dark tower, the V lit up like a bright red scar.

"What's a good answer for this? How can we fight it?" he shouted into the black mouth of earth. "We opened our mouths and welcomed them here with open arms, helped them build the very thing that would kill us." He turned to Rachel. "Some things you build, not so easy to tear down again. Now, what's the answer for that?"

The wind carried his cry through the air, and the question rested in the darkness around them, in the limbs of the tree. And something else waited under the roots of the trees and beneath their feet. The wind rippled through the leaves, shook the maple's branches in answer. Loaded with emerald and red-orange cicadas, the branches swayed as the insects split their skins and struggled out. As the ground shook, they emerged from the dark, wet earth, emerged after a lifetime of waiting alone. Night after night, they had awakened. Wave upon wave, they came.

"The ground gon' sour?" Rachel asked as she opened Big Daddy's passenger door.

"Not the ground. Us."

The humming rose, a hymn that seemed to sing the world anew. Up from the jagged edge of earth, a great figure climbed out, six gigantic, jointed legs lifting it up and out of the land Doc and his people had once proudly claimed as their own. Iridescent wings unfolded from its wide, curved back. They glistened and sparkled in the night, unearthing mountains of soil and roots and old things not witnessed since the angel poured its first bowl over the sun, and the moon had opened like a great eye in the sky. Free from its dark sleep, the giant unfurled its wings and thrummed a deep tympani-drum sound that the little ones echoed and joined in, their song a bellowing in the air.

Rachel and Doc covered their ears and watched in wonder as it raised its great, jewel-encrusted head and turned to them. It seemed as if a million eyes watched them from all directions, all at once; then within minutes, the creature stomped across acres of what had once been the town's most fertile land. The ground shook beneath its many feet, and the others raised their drumsong as it headed toward the Viscerol plant.

Safe in Big Daddy, Rachel and Doc stared at each other, not speaking in the airless truck. They held each other for a long, long time, and for an even longer time, it seemed like neither one of them breathed. Then they jumped, a startled, delayed reaction after they heard the thunder, a rush of mighty wings as the last of the Viscerol plant and its signature water tower crashed to the ground. The earth rumbled one final time, and Rachel and Doc shook in the truck that rattled like a great tin can. The wind howled, a loud keening, and the old trees lay low, then all was still and quiet, and the only thing they could see was the white mouth of the moon.

Rachel rolled the window down, hands shaking, the old handle squeaking. She started to crank the truck up, but Doc reached for the keys.

"Come on out and let me drive, girl," he said.

Tired as she was, Rachel didn't even have the strength to argue. She just shook her head and looked at him. "Daddy, you ain't driven Big Daddy in years."

Doc wiped a layer of gossamer threads from around his jaw and his throat. His hands looked smooth, sturdy. His heart felt ripe and strong. "When I leave, you leave," he said. "Step on out, Slick Bean, and let's get up out of here."

Rachel stared at him, her eyes wide with wonder. "Doc?"

He hummed a happy tune as they drove off, some of that old country music Rachel pretended she couldn't stand. Big Daddy groaned down the road; only empty shells and withering husks left behind. But above them and around them, hidden in the dark earth and in the green branches of trees, something like hope remained, listening and waiting for a warm spring night and a mischievous wind to return again.

Before the River Knew

Before the river knew its name, before the hummingbird dipped its beak in crimson bloom, there was a humming. A golden light coiled tight as a spring, beneath the earth's dark skin. The whisper of honey, the scent of rain on sunbaked clay. A rhythm, deep as the drum's first beat, pulsing in the heartwood of the world. Then, a shattering. Not of glass, but of silence. A pouring forth, like molten gold, a laughter that shook the very roots of the baobab. The first shimmer, the first flash of copper in the sun's eye. The river, suddenly knowing its course.

Mama told me stories of a woman born of water and light. Not born, exactly, but unfurling, like a fern in the first spring rain. She carried the sun in her smile, they say, and the moon in the curve of her hip. Her hair, a river of ebony, braided with stars. She walked the earth, barefoot, and wherever her toes touched, flowers bloomed. Not the pale, fragile kind, but the kind that smelled of spice and magic. Mama said she taught the women how to weave their dreams into indigo cloth, how to sing the songs that called the rain down. She said this woman, this shimmering, golden woman, lives in us still.

Dirt beneath my nails, the crescent smell of wet earth. Grandmama's hands, rough as bark, trace lines on my palm. "This," she said, "is the river's path. This," she whispered, "is the place where she rose." Not from the sea, like some say, but from the heart of the earth itself. A great geyser of light, a song that birthed the rainbow. She wore a crown of cowrie shells, each one a story whispered on the wind. She taught us the language of the fireflies and cicadas, the language of the bees, the secrets of the herbs and spice, the trees. She showed us how to find the gold in our own veins. Grandmama said her name, like a river, flows through us all.

River, Clap Your Hands

Night

All night long, the weary sound of water dripped from the roof into the bucket below, eroding her dreams. Ava woke from a sleep that bore her like an ocean, her mind still filled with the raindrop drum. The moon had veiled its face so that the stars could not see her cry. She woke and saw the street alive. She remembered when the neighborhood was submerged. She remembered when she was ruined by waters, ruined and resurrected by waters that bore spent seeds, the corpses of trees, and times that would never come again. Neither born nor named, time swam lifeless inside her, and the lifeless tides swam with her. Ava touched damp garments that clung to her skin, close as guilt.

Watching the early morning walkers with their dogs at their sides, Ava was reminded that she lived among a people who believed in seasons. She lived among those who believed in the story and the song, among people who believed in prayer. Yet she knew nothing but the language of loss in a landscape she no longer recognized.

Ava rubbed her palm across the empty bowl of her stomach. Now she longed for the days when she had felt full, when the nausea filled her and all she could taste was the salt from the stale crackers she nibbled on. Longing gnawed at her brain, consumed her waking thoughts. She never had the chance to hold it.

Rain

Rain made her anxious. The river swelling outside beyond the bluff filled Ava with dread. The rain fell faster, harder than it had last night. Outside, the walkers had long since scattered. Only the hardcore remained, refused to retreat. All was a sheet of gray steel. Inside, her mind was pitch black, except the brief flashes of light that stung the sky of memory. The couple who came for her, flashlights in hand, the beams reflecting off the violent waters that careened outside her door. Paralyzed, her body was caught in between. Trapped between a birth and a transformation. The old house had become a ship, tossed along the siren's song. Long after, terror filled her, even on the brightest days, flashbacks of all that she had lost. She was weary, tired of losing what she'd never had.

"Maybe it's a blessing," Grandmama said. "Maybe the Lord didn't want you to have that child. Birthing in the middle of all that strife. The Lord spared him." Grandmama was convinced the child was a boy.

"You carrying that baby mighty low," she had said. But that was then, before the first gills came.

"Sometimes, I wish He had spared me."

Grandmama sucked in air, a tone to freeze eardrums. Her eyes were cool water.

Wine

She had loved him. Most nights Ava told herself she had. She missed the way his fingers traced her flesh, the way his eyes widened, marveling at her smooth palms and their missing lifelines. She remembered him tracing the curve of throat, him lingering there until she could not breathe, the simple pleasure before his tongue found the gills. He had drawn away as if her touch had stung him. She never would forget his fear staring back at her, pupils dilated in widening circles, receding like the ripples in the river, him pulling away like the tide of the sea.

That night she drank red merlot, glass after cheap glass, and listened to Aretha, feeling like everything but a *natural woman.* That night her mind was all rivulets and rock pools. She spent the evening ruminating, returning to the same eye of water. Ava added three teardrops of pokeroot to her glass, and felt her throat constrict and release. Grandmama's rootwork. She always had a recipe, but nothing could fix this—heartbreak. The flesh had grown raw and itchy inside, a wound that would not heal. Suddenly a soul in the lost and found didn't sound so unnatural to her. She had felt more than good inside, more possible with him. Now she felt undone, in flux. She was turned inside out. It was some time after the third or fourth glass, when the wine dribbled down her chin like ruby drops of blood, that she realized it was not his absence she mourned. It was the willful blindness that his presence helped her hide. Now how would she hide from herself?

Bridges

When Ava was a child her mother recited poems to her. Fierce poems of fault lines, of rivers turned, of a great tortoise whose back was as wide as the river's hips, of ancient paths lost and regained. They would emerge from beneath the Old Bridge. Together they dried themselves on the river's shore and watched the two trains running overhead. The air stung. It would take hours for Ava to perfect the rhythm of breathing. Sometimes drifters would leave piles of driftwood, old bottles, used cans. Her mother would make a fire and with a stick she would carve old signs and symbols in the soil. On those cool, mosquito-filled nights, Ava swatted flies and was warmed by her mother's company. Comforted by her mother's voice, her gills receded into her flesh, disappeared with the wind.

Mama kept her secrets close. Tight as water skins. "The Old Bridge is not the first bridge. Another lies in the water below," Mama had said, motioning with her hand. The thin membrane of webbing had finally dried and dropped away. It lay in scaly piles in the sand. "The first bridge was the river's spine, the Great Turtle. Our people swam across it, drifting finally into these waters. The first people we met lived up there, high on the hills." The high bluffs of the quiet river city were Ava's first glimpse of what would later become her home. Mama kept her secrets close. Ava learned this when she woke and discovered that she was alone. Mama had left her sleeping on the river's bank.

Hunger

When the river came alive, it hungered. It grew teeth and rose from its banks, swallowed the parks, the bending paths, the abandoned cars, the empty lots filled with broken glass, and encircled the bone yard, and the house. Ava woke to the sound of water running, like a faucet left on, and at first she thought it was a dream. She often dreamed of the river, the banks where her mother left her all those years ago, before the tall fishing man discovered her weeping by the still smoldering fire, before he took her home where she met Grandmama. But when Ava opened her eyes, she realized the water had joined her, and that if she did not rise it would cover her and all the room. Then the cramps came; thunder deep below her chest. The baby, it was coming too soon. The water had awakened it. The water called to them both. Ava felt the gills open on her neck, the skin lengthen and stretch between her fingers. She needed to get out of the water, she needed to resist its call. Trapped between the birth and her own transformation, she climbed onto the top of the desk, then took a breath, plunged into the water's oily depths, swam out the door, in search of Grandmama.

Hearts

It was the blame in their eyes that made Ava shun their company. The silent accusation made her huddle in the staging area on her own. People wanted to know why, couldn't understand how. The mayor said to go. Staying wasn't part of anyone's plan. "Why?" was the question that rested on everyone's lips. Why did Ava and so many others decide to ride out the storm? How could they not know the storm would ride them?

Grandmama once told Ava that her husband's heart had just stopped. "It knew Amp wasn't gon' never quit working, so his heart just revolted against itself." She said she found him lying on the floor he had lain down himself. "He came from a people who always used their hands. Sometimes," she said, "against themselves. But not my Amp. He built this house when we married, built it before your daddy was even born. I guess it's good he didn't know his boy wasn't gon' live long as him. In his way your daddy's heart revolted, too. Sometimes it ain't good to love so much in this world." For Ava and Grandmama, the house and its memories were all that they had left.

To keep the house when her husband died, Grandmama cleaned cracked china and porcelain bowls, shined broken mirrors and windows that stayed closed. Her hands cooked meals for dinners she was never invited to, graced tables with straightback chairs where she could not sit. Where she worked she heard haints in the halls and would return in time to make Ava's late-night dinners, telling her stories that left her amused, enthralled. She complained that there was nothing truly alive in some of those other, grander houses, the walls had veins with no blood in them.

Grandmama said a house has got to breathe, got to have some soul and a little laughter to make its foundation stay strong, said not every house, not every family can carry the weight. She said what Ava and she shared made their home more beautiful, more sacred than the fanciest castle. Ava believed her, too, right up until the water came and took her past and future, her home and her baby.

Loss

Long after they lost their house in the flood, after they moved to another river city, Grandmama stood in line with hollow-faced folks. Worried and weary, she waited like the others to get her pills. The churches collected toothpaste and brushes, brought clothing and prayers. The kindness made the loss less sharp. The city's humid heat made them feel less naked. "But feeling clean don't help me sleep," Grandmama said. The water haunted her dreams, too. So she waited and swallowed pills she knew by color, tried to muster up an appetite to eat. Grandmama missed her garden and her homemade cha cha. Ava missed her baby.

Pain

When Ava found Grandmama, she was upstairs still asleep in her bed. The look on her face was pure disbelief. She refused to leave the house without getting herself dressed. "I'm not going with all my business hanging out," she cried. "If the Lord gonna take me, I am at least going to have on my good dress." The pain in Ava's face made her stop. "What's the matter, child?"

"The baby," Ava managed. "It's coming, I can't stop it."

"Stop calling that boy 'it' and come help me pull down this ladder." The water was rising up the steps. Framed photos, dishes, and books floated just below them. It took all Ava's strength to help her Grandmama up into the attic. The pains came so strong, she wanted to lie down in the murky water and let the flood carry her wherever it willed.

"Come on, Ava," her Grandmama said, reaching for her. They waited in the attic, darkness all around them. "We in God's hands now."

Air

While the water rose and their lone flashlight faded, Grandmama hummed and sang. She began with the stories Ava had heard as a child, the ones that told of a people who came from water, who lived and breathed it, the way the others swallowed air. The infant Ava had loved and feared rested in a worn sheet between them. Its skin felt smooth and warm to Ava's touch, but she knew when Grandmama first held it, that there was something wrong. The child, a boy, never took its first breath.

It was Grandmama who heard the people screaming below. She called back, thankful already though they had not yet been delivered. Racked with pain so deep it seemed to sear her belly, Ava managed to rise from grief, the blood slick and running down her knees. She took the flashlight and knocked out a hole in the roof. With each strike, the rain came faster, her tears harder.

"We're here," Grandmama shouted. Ava did not wait for the reply below. As Grandmama stood up, widening the hole with her shoulders and waving to the couple in the boat, Ava took the silent child, caressed its little winged limbs and released it into the water and the night. It was dark; later they would need a flashlight just to see the food they ate, but then, hovering in the house that was once her shelter, all Ava wanted was to see her child's face. For a moment Ava thought she saw the tiny body shudder as the water covered it. Inside she felt her heart revolt. *He came from a people who always used their hands. Sometimes against themselves.* Ava turned away, her face full of tears.

"What did you do?" Grandmama cried. Her eyes were fetid floodwaters, her voice cold enough to stop a heart.

Silence

The house they loved was a waterlogged corpse, but the city was not all they had left behind. Something had changed. The water between them had darkened and risen like the river and the flood. They spoke in clipped sentences. Grandmama slept as much as she could, while Ava dreamed awake. She replayed each second of memory, trying to recall if she had imagined the infant wriggling, picturing if and how the child might have lived.

Thirst

The night rain came and invaded her sleep as stealthily as the night of the hurricane, Ava woke with a hangover and one question on her mind. She flung the coverlet back, placed one bare foot on the hardwood floor. Stood in the open door, wearing her good slip, wrinkled and wine-stained. She took a deep breath, inhaled the rain and the sun-shower air.

Grandmama had answered her call on the first ring.

Now, after making their way to the river's bank, Ava slipped out of her shoes, stepped into the muddy water. The river whispered around her ankles and her feet.

"Listen," Grandmama said. The weeds and trees swayed behind her. "The river is trying to tell you something: move, change. If your mama hadn't gotten lost, if she had stuck to another plan, she never would have met your father." Grandmama bent and picked up the shoes, wiped loose soil from the soles. "Here, at the riverside, is where they began. When she left the last time, she knew your daddy would return to the same place where he first met her. She knew he would never stop searching, never stop remembering. Sometimes it's dangerous to love that much."

Ava peeled off her dress and stood in the open air, the wind brushing her nipples, still plump with mother's milk. Her daddy had said she had her mother's face, strong bones, wide nose, wider forehead. Moon-marked, Grandmama had said, so she kept her in the sun. The closer Ava got to the river, the less air her lungs needed to breathe. She felt dizzy, her skin tingled and writhed with thirst. "Being lost helped us find you, Ava. You always thought the river took something from you, took your mama away, broke your daddy's heart, but maybe the river gave you something more."

Skin that was once dark and burnished now took on a copper-like sheen. Scales that were barely detectible appeared more pronounced. Ava began to walk into the waters, not far from the strip of sand where her mother had once told her lies and read her poems.

"I'm not mad, Grandmama, not anymore," Ava said. She unraveled the thick French braids she wore. Her hair puffed around her shoulders in a dark, wavy cloud. "I just need to try to find him. I know what I saw, know what I felt. I think he's alive."

Grandmama waved away a witch doctor that hovered near her ear. "If you're going, you need to listen to the river when you can't hear me. She ain't going to tell you nothing wrong. Listen to her now. She is telling you that there ain't no shame in changing. Baby, you are what you are. You come from this here water, but you also are part of this land. All them years I tried to keep you safe from this"—Grandmama pointed at the Mississippi—"but when I wasn't looking, the river come to take you back anyway. So find what you love most from both of those things that make you, and then you go on out in this world and make yourself."

Ava walked deeper into the shallow water, felt the river whispering, pulling all around her. Grandmama clutched the blue sandals, crushed the sundress to her chest. "You don't want to listen to me, then go ahead, listen to the river. It's been calling you since you were born. The water is wise. When you feel there ain't no other way, do like this river do and bend."

Grandmama stood away from the water, heels planted in the sandbar, as if she was afraid the river would rise and take her, too. Unwilling to leave on bad terms, but unable to stay now that they were good, Ava rushed out of the water to give her Grandmama one final hug.

And then, as if the sky had waited for this moment, the rain stopped. The only echo was Grandmama's whispered "Be good, girl. I hope to be here when you come back" and the hush of the river wind. Ava took a deep breath, inhaled the last of the sun-shower air. Humidity wrapped around her ankles, pulled her closer to the bank.

Sunlight shimmered
on the brown river's surface
the gold mermaid smiled

Forrest

One man built a ladder
of stacked up black bones
to climb the living dead
to rise above his own salvation.
He wanted muscle and limbs
blood and wombs, wanted to reach
above the dark soil to become a god

But his mouth was a scar
and his chest a deep hole
there was no heart in him.

The scar and the hole
carried him through
the great war that was
a cleaving. He fell through
a door in the earth, fell
straight through the unhealed
line of history.

The black bones heard his cries
bellowing across the dry husk
of fields and the scar led his two feet
across the broken stalks and the rocks.

His voice was what the children
heard in their dreams, those sold
off, far from their mother's breast.
His voice was the beast that
growled behind the lightning
and the cold that rained down
from the sky.

And the men, whose bones
he picked, and the women, whose
marrow he sucked, wailed his
name in the wind. And the sound
filled the air above the old stone
monuments, as if a song and a prayer
were paths their lives could follow
back to land.

And the children, blessed children
the arm babies and the knee ones,
the not quite lost their baby fat ones
shimmered in the air, drifting like
black dandelion seedlings
above the red dust.

Once on the cobblestone path
along the river, I heard a terrible moan
and I stood back to see what the dead
might bring, but no sorrow walked
out of the dark water.

No weeping of rotted flesh
or clumps of pain-soaked hair

no haints shining like a prophet
climbing from the river banks
with a vision too unholy to tell.

Instead, driftwood, an old tree
bent like an outstretched hand
hope floating across the waters.
The future traveled
past the endless journey of fear
ancestors calling from the deep
returning from the far reaches
where men once dreamed the world flat
and time dreamed it round again.

Sweet Chariots in Dixieland

When we take these things that are our own,
and develop them until they are finer things,
that's pure culture.
—W.C. Handy

SWING-LO HUNG FROM THE gnarled branches of an oak tree, his jaws working a wad of Juicy Fruit. He spat the gum out, then jumped down, his short legs pumping as he trotted over in new sneakers to where Darius stood, leaning against the base of the monument. The bronze statue gleamed dully in the afternoon sun. Darius crooked his arm a little, avoiding a pile of bird shit. A few blocks away, he could hear the music festival in full swing and the trolley clanging down Main Street. The scent of magnolias filled the park.

"Who the fuck is Nathan Bedford Forrest?"

Swing-Lo frowned and removed his glasses, then stooped to squint at the plaque. The statue was green and rusty at its base. Swing-Lo wrinkled his nose and sneezed, then wiped his hands on his jeans.

"General Nathan Bedford Forrest," he read, "1821–1877. Led the Army of Tennessee in the Secession, January 28, 1861." He shrugged and rose slowly, replacing his glasses.

"Some damn cracka don't nobody remember. Who give a fuck?" The words sounded cooler when Darius said them.

Darius smirked as Swing-Lo mouthed the words silently, *damn, cracka, fuck.* Darius didn't know it, but sometimes Swing-Lo practiced in the mirror, in the mornings when he brushed his teeth. He kept the cold water running so his Grandmama Dessie wouldn't hear him. He hid the soap just in case.

"Boy, what you whisperin' 'bout?"

Darius had climbed all the way to the top of Forrest's head. He sat with his sneakers drumming against the general's enormous bronze ears.

"Yo mama!" The two boys grinned. Swing-Lo dropped his glasses into his pocket, then scrambled to join his friend. His new shoes slipped on the smooth surface. Swing-Lo sucked his teeth and dug his heel into Forrest's crotch, then plopped down under the general's chin.

Four girls skipped past General Forrest with two ropes in hand. One with a head full of braids jumped over a black cannon. Her colorful beads rattled in the air. The others yelped and followed suit, leaping over the pair of cannons like hurdles. A fifth one hurried to catch up, ponytails swaying in the wind.

Five blacks, two ropes: double-dutch.

Swing-Lo and Darius whistled appreciatively.

#

Minnie watched the children from a bench in Confederate Park, her back to the river, the shopping cart parked at her side. She sucked a peppermint and batted the piece of candy with the tip of her tongue, allowing the cool mint to sink into her mouth. *Them younguns tickle me to death*, she thought. The whistling boys had nudged an old memory awake, a pleasant one. One of them backwater tunes. She pulled the guitar from the plastic trash bag resting at her feet and stared at its worn finish. The backing was scratched and now only the words "sun go down" remained. *Too many years on the road.* Her mind was too old to recall the song's name right off. She figured it was older than all the children put together. Minnie adjusted the guitar and hoped her fingers would remember.

She swallowed the last of the peppermint and then began to sing. *Good morning, blues, please shake hands with me.* Her voice drifted across the park. *I said, good morning, blues, please shake hands with me.* Two men snapping photos stopped to listen. *I've got the blues this morning, just as low as I can be.*

Her voice was a blackgummed burst of accents, all bantu-chickasaw-scotch-irish-mississippi-delta rolled into one. Oh, *the blues got ways sometimes, just like a natural man.* The words dropped from her lips like broken bits of calabash, *Oh, the blues got ways sometimes just like a natural man,* split like walnuts in the August sun. *I don't care which away you turn,* Minnie tapped her feet in time, *they always is on your hands.* Nimble fingers stroked the guitar lovingly. Minnie closed her eyes and hummed, felt the blues welling up from the base of her belly.

Swing-Lo and Darius smiled and exchanged glances, straddling Forrest.

Minnie heard a few voices around her, but she shut them out and kept singing the blues. She heard only the music and the way folks hollered appreciation in the dusty juke joints of her youth. The music carried her there and she tried to sing like she did when people called her Memphis Minnie.

She was born Minerva Lizzie Mae Douglas, but she dropped the family names when she reached Beale Street, fresh from Sweetwater, Mississippi. She had been calling herself Minnie since she was a small girl, a "youngun" not much older than those sweet mannish boys or the little girls that stared curiously at her now. Little girls weren't so fast then, but then again, Minnie didn't stay little for long.

Good morning, blues, please shake my hand. Minnie finished the song and raised heavy lids to see a circle of smiling faces.

"Hey, Ma'am! Hey, Miss Ma'am!" Darius waved his arms and leapt from Forrest's head. Swing-Lo climbed down to follow him, inching one foot behind the other. He didn't want to break his neck or, worse, his glasses.

Swing-Lo caught up with Darius. The two boys pushed their way through the circle of girls. A tall one with a tiny gap in her front teeth glared at them. Darius stuck his tongue out and ducked out of reach. The children grew silent when two men in golf shirts and chinos stumbled forward. Minnie could smell them before they opened their mouths.

"Oh, *die blues sangerine,"* the fat one cried in a German accent. A fancy camera hung from a strap around his neck. The neon wristband strained against his meaty wrist. *Festival must be jumpin, early today,* Minnie thought, clutching her guitar close to her.

"*Blues sangerine*, sing us a song,' the second man said, more gently. He hiccupped. "We've come all the way from Munich and we want to hear some blues. The real blues. There's only us in the clubs." He nodded toward Beale Street. A map of Graceland fluttered in his hand.

"No, no, negerine," the heavier man cried. "Sing us 'Dixie!' Sing us 'Dixie' and one of those negerine spirituals!"

Minnie felt her pulse quicken. Out of the corner of her eye she could see the two boys fidgeting.

"Awww man, you hear that shit?" the tall one asked. "I guess she s'posed to be Aunt Jemima now." His skinny legs reminded Minnie of Sunnyland Slim back in Georgia.

"Whose aunt is Jemima?" asked a girl holding a rope.

The short boy in the glasses poked her with his elbow. "Hush up!" he said in a loud voice. The girls snickered as Slim punched Li'l Bit in the shoulder.

Minnie gave the tourists a long steady look, studied their beer-shiny eyes and their pale, pasty faces beaded with sweat. Then she looked from them to the children's faces. Slim and L'il Bit frowned.

She winked at them, but the boys looked confused. My, oh, my, Minnie thought, been a mighty long time since I had me a "special request."

The tourists waited, grinning. It looked as if the war memorials leaned forward expectantly.

Minnie pushed back the anger and looked beyond it, surprised herself and discovered that she wanted to sing *Swing low, sweet chariot.* Minnie did not know why she chose these lyrics, *Coming for to carry me home,* but she sang them as if they were the only ones she had ever known. *I'm sometimes up and sometimes down.* Minnie sang, feeling the lyrics, deciding that they were hers. *But still my soul feels heavenly bound. Coming for to carry me home.* She felt her way slowly through the words, filling them up as a silence swept the park.

When she finished, she saw that the men no longer smiled. The children, including Slim and Li'l Bit, were wide-eyed, as if they had just learned what "spirituals" meant, or why they got to stay home from school on January 15, or why some folks didn't eat BBQ on the Fourth of July.

The men clapped, astonished. Fat Man had tears in his eyes, and Minnie was surprised to find a few of her own. She sucked them in, remembering that she had not sang a spiritual since she was baptized in Sweetwater. Would Gina have understood this feeling, she wondered? The quiet dignity, the power in a song that had once been chains? Then she noticed the gentleman digging in his pocket. *I know he ain't*, she thought, narrowing her eyes.

Gentleman saw Minnie's scowl and quickly stuffed the bills back into his pocket. "Thank you, Miss," he said, his eyes bouncing everywhere but on Minnie's face. The children watched him curiously. "That was lovely. Just lovely," he said, his voice wavering as he herded Fat Man away. Fat Man glanced once over his shoulder. His eyes were wet and shining.

When the tourist departed, the children drifted away, returning to their horseplay and jump ropes, all save one.

"Why you gat that scar on yo' face?"

The ponytailed girl sat on the bench beside Minnie, her legs swinging. She was wearing ankle socks, the frilly kind. *Somebody must look after her,* Minnie thought, smiling. *She gat enough oil on her legs to fill a tank.*

Minnie was slow to answer, her mind rejecting words that might be too harsh. She searched for a response, but her thoughts were still jumbled from what had just happened. That's why Minnie loved the blues. They came easily—sometimes too easily. Finding the right words was a different matter.

Minnie watched a gray squirrel scurry across the path. It disappeared into a magnolia tree.

"Honey, scars are just a part of living," she said after a spell. "You can't get through this life without at least some scars. Better this li'l one on the outside," she brushed her fingertips across the pink mark, "than big ones on the inside."

The girl thought for a long silence, her little face somber. For a minute Minnie worried. *Maybe I said too much.* She didn't want to scare the child. *But hell,* Minnie thought. She didn't know if she even understood this herself.

Then PonyTail smiled.

Gina, Minnie thought. The girl was quite pretty. *Just like my Gina. Poor child left with her grandmama.* Minnie drifted back in Sweetwater, back to them other days. At one time she had thought the blues would make a home for her and Gina, but she soon learned that the blues was no place for little girls. Home. Minnie looked over at her basket and the plastic bag at her feet. She thought about that word, home, and what it now meant: nothing.

A breeze drifted through the bag, making it billow softly. The guitar, Gina, rested in Minnie's lap, the only thing of value she owned. PonyTail scratched her knee, flicking a red ant into the grass. Minnie dug into her pocket and fished out a green-and-white-striped peppermint. PonyTail beamed and scooped the candy out of Minnie's palm. The little girl stooped to tighten her shoelaces, then sprang to her feet.

"Thank you ma'am," she said in a singsong voice and skipped away, humming. *Step on a crack, break yo' mama's back.*

"Honey, you welcome." Minnie nodded and waved goodbye, cradling Gina. Her thoughts drifted down the river.

#

The next day Minnie made the trip to St. Augustine's soup kitchen. "Kessler, they had *tears* in their eyes."

Minnie stood in line talking to the man in front of her, a lunch tray in her hands. She picked up a few napkins and put the extra ones back. She noticed he was wearing a new hat.

"You know, they never clean this silverware," he said, trading one spoon for another. He held the new spoon up to his eye. "Did you check your spoon?"

"Yeah, but did you hear me? I said, I haven't felt that good singing since I left Chicago with—"

"Kansas City Joe," Kessler added hastily. He placed a carton of fruit cocktail on his tray, then shuffled two steps ahead to inspect the sandwiches.

"I tell you, they thought they had me in a trick bag, but the more I sang, the better I felt. It was like those old spirituals was lifting me up." Minnie grabbed the fruit cocktail and the tuna fish. "But you know what? I turned the tables on 'em. Hell, I done clowned with the best of 'em."

Kessler waited while she went back to replace her spoon. They took their trays over to an empty table. Minnie could see her shopping cart parked outside the window of the church annex.

"So you played the fool for a few tourists today. What else is new?" Kessler asked, sipping lemonade from a white styrofoam cup. He made a face. It was too sweet.

"What's new? What's new is that I felt good for a change. Useful. I wasn't singing just to be singing. It started that way. Hell, I could have cussed both of them out, but then all those children . . ." Minnie shook her head. "You should have seen those kids' faces. The way they looked when ole Memphis Minnie to' it up."

Kessler rolled his eyes, swallowed slowly. "You want that cocktail?" Minnie handed it to him.

"I wasn't just some old bag lady then, and I wasn't no, no . . ." Minnie searched for the word. "Hell, I don't know what they said, but we gat more words for black folks than you can shake a stick at."

Kessler chuckled. "Tell me about it."

"I guess you would know," Minnie said, grinning. "But it was like I was—"

"An old fool."

Minnie chewed more slowly.

"What?" Kessler asked, exasperated. "Minnie, I'm tired of seeing you do this. Every few months you start working yourself up over some kind of *meshuggina,* saying you're going to make a comeback. But how long are you going to kid yourself? You're not going to make a comeback. Not now, not ever, and that little girl you've been looking for, she's gone."

Minnie stared at Kessler for what seemed like the longest time. She didn't chew or swallow. It was as if the tuna fish stuck in her throat. After a while she quietly wrapped her half-eaten sandwich in a napkin and shoved it into her pocket. Then she gently pushed her tray away and stood up.

"Now where are you going?" Kessler's voice sounded annoyed and apologetic.

Minnie trudged through the doors and did not answer.

#

For a long time Minnie's gaze lingered on the children, their shouts and giggles echoing among the statues as they played hide-and-seek. She tossed a few crumbs of bread onto the sidewalk, watched the pigeons waddle over to the scattered bits. Gina was tucked safely in the plastic bag, shoved at the bottom of her shopping cart. It was almost sunset and the river shone bright orange. Most evenings Minnie took Gina down to the railroad tracks at the bottom of the hill. There she would play a little and enjoy the view of the river. Today her heart felt harder than General Forrest's head.

"Girl, don't you fall out of that tree!" The child, no more than six, was perched in the branches of an oak.

"Got you!" Sunnyland Slim tapped the girl's leg and sprinted off.

Minnie shook her head. *I don't know how these kids can stand to rip and run all day. Li'l selves ought to be somewhere tired.* It seemed as if Minnie had always been tired during her youth. Her earliest memory was hearing the blues ring out over the cotton fields before she ran away. But even as a young woman, Minnie had grown weary of her life as an aspiring country blues singer. It wasn't easy. The rambling schedule, the dusty roads, and the hollow laughter that sounded the same no matter what town she swung through wore her down to the bone. That's why she dropped everything, including her baby Regina and the last few dollars she earned down in Georgia, so she could follow Kansas City Joe to Chicago.

Minnie looked out at the children playing in the park, their innocent joy a sharp contrast to her own hard-won weariness, and hoped none of them would grow up to be as naive as her. She had thought if she could cut a record or two, she could stay off the road a bit and raise Gina the right way, the way a real mother should. But the deal with Columbia fell through and Minnie left Chicago broke and disillusioned. And she wasn't the only one who had left the city with a few more blues and one scar more than she had bargained for. Chicago had sucked her down like the last bit of peppermint.

Minnie returned to Memphis with the intent of resuming her life with Gina, but by the time she sobered long enough to put the bottle down, she learned her mama had died in Sweetwater and her Gina was gone.

Minnie watched the children, a faint smile touching her lips as she recognized a few of them from the other day.

"Hey Miss Ma'am!" the tall one shouted. Minnie waved back at him. *I see Slim and Li'l Bit still cuttin' up*, she thought and wondered why that spiritual had moved her so. If the truth was told, she knew she'd stopped really singing, from the heart, when that deal with Columbia fell through. That man at the Flamingo Room had tried to get her back on the marquee. *What was his name?* Minnie couldn't remember. She knew that he had promised her a raise and a new sequin costume. Said it didn't matter if she wasn't on a 45, said she had left Memphis and that alone gave her star appeal. That's what he said. Star appeal. Sooey at Pee Wee's Saloon thought the scar would be good for business, but neither of them understood.

Minnie's eyes followed the children as they tumbled over the weathered statue in their uninhibited play. She knew that it had been a long time since she'd cared about her career or how she looked. By the time the train carried her across the Mason-Dixie line, Minnie had lost all interest in the blues. She tried for a while, but when she got on stage, heart bursting with all them new blues, she just didn't feel the hope anymore.

Sometimes Minnie would look out from the smoky stage and see just as many white faces as the black ones. Minnie knew you didn't need melanin to understand the blues. That was the problem with most folks; they didn't understand that you didn't have to have rhythm or know how to dance or be born in the Delta to know the blues. The blues wasn't about sorrow or misery. They were about hope. That was something all people knew a little about, but Minnie had returned to Memphis with everything but that.

The sound of the Main Street trolley echoed in the park. Minnie looked up and saw that all the children had gone, leaving her alone with the statue. *Nathan, you looking bout as mean as I'm feeling,* she thought and chuckled. She slapped her knee, thinking of those tourists. *And Lord, them younguns must've thought I was crazy, singing them old slave songs.* Her body shook with laughter as the tears rolled down her eyes. "Swing low sweet chariot . . ." The words hung in the twilight, a ghost of comfort. Minnie's gaze fell on Gina, the guitar, tucked safely in her basket. She thought of the sweetness she'd once dreamed for her daughter, the home the blues couldn't provide. What would Gina truly make of this world, this city, these symbols of division? How could Minnie, her mother, make sense of it for her? Then, as if little Gina had whispered it in her ear, Minnie got an idea. She stopped laughing. The crinkles around her mouth disappeared. She saw the children's faces when the drunk men made fun of her and then she saw how they looked when she sang with all the sadness and dignity she could muster.

Lord, them kids don't know nothing bout the blues, she thought, hesitating, and yet, when she sang, something inside them clicked. If li'l kids and foreigners could feel that old music, Minnie wondered, then what about the rest of these grown folks?

Minnie dug into her pocket and fished out another peppermint. She had plenty to think about. She popped the candy into her mouth, humming quietly.

#

"Give me all your Confederate flags."

The woman behind the counter peered at Minnie over her glasses, the signature giant pair of overalls taking up the whole wall over her shoulder. Her eyes scanned Minnie's neat, if not spotless, attire, then rested on the pile of bills before her. Minnie waited patiently while the clerk at A. Schwaab's made up her mind to serve her.

It was lunch time and the aisles were crowded with tourists. They perused the shelves, waving at each other from across the room with bottles of "Voodoo Love Potion," "Indian Money," and "Mojo Magic" in their hands. Overhead, the pair of size 60 overalls hung from two hooks as if their owner had hung them to dry. Minnie couldn't imagine who would wear them.

"Honey, it's green, so give me all you gat." The clerk narrowed her eyes, but after some hesitation, she disappeared. A few minutes later, she returned with an arm full of flags. She dropped them heavily on the counter next to a pair of bamboo Chinese fans. A few flags fluttered to the floor. Minnie bent down to scoop them up, breathing heavily. She didn't let the woman's rudeness bother her. *I know what tune you'll be singing soon.* But that would have to wait. Minnie concentrated on getting that flag she saw tumble near the tie rack. She reached for it with a shaking hand but a pudgy little boy, no more than three years old, stepped on it.

"Todd, come here right this minute."

Todd groaned and followed his mother, but Minnie saw that his sneakers had made a track. She left the ruined flag on the floor and leaned over the counter, rasping, "Give me your bumper stickers."

The clerk looked as if she would protest, then glanced at Minnie's face and thought better of it. Minnie smiled and thanked the woman fifteen minutes later, when she shuffled through the door, bags filled with every flag, sticker, button, pin, bandana, hat, T-shirt, and piece of Confederate paraphernalia conceivable.

She dropped them in the shopping basket she had parked outside the store, then whistled "Dixie" all the way down Beale Street.

#

Kessler slammed his cup of Kool-Aid on the table when he looked out the window and saw Minnie parking her loot outside the soup kitchen. He had not seen her in over a week.

"What the hell do you need all that for?" he asked.

"I'm going to make me a new costume."

"A costume? Out of Confederate flags? It's August, Elvis time, not Halloween. Minnie, have you been drinking?"

Minnie drew a button from her pocket and handed it to Kessler. It read "Born a Rebel." She eyed his lemon cookie and reached for it. Kessler dropped the button and gently smacked her hand away. "You know the rules. Get your own. I stood my ass in line, so get to it."

Minnie smiled and watched the others thank the volunteers for the cookies and sandwiches. She wasn't going to let Old Kessler ruin her day.

"I knew you'd go bonkers," he said, passing her the cookie on a napkin, "out there carrying all those blues with you, but why would you trade them for those worthless chatzkas?"

"Worthless?" Minnie said, chewing. Jackson's lemon cookies were heavenly. "Honey, that basket is full of gold."

"Don't tell me you're trying to sell them? I mean, who would buy them from you?" Kessler looked incredulous, as if he were trying to imagine a "rebel" walking up to purchase the "gold" from Minnie.

"I don't need the money."

"Yeah, right." Kessler scraped the mayo off his baloney and bit in.

"The way I see it, I'm Southern and my blood is in this soil, too." Kessler nodded between bites. "They gat that Confederate flag flying over the State Capitol, so I'm going to take it and whistle me some Dixie. Hell, the Confederates actually did manage to scrape together a black regiment, though they never saw no action."

Kessler looked skeptical. Minnie rubbed the shiny orange button with her thumb.

"Kessler, the folks I know grew up hating that flag. They hated that flag and the way certain folks would always pull out certain things. You know what I'm talkin' about, 'Old Man River,' 'Gone with the Wind,' anything to remind them and us just how precious we are, once property. I want to know who said everything has to stay ugly? Ain't we tired of this? When we all gon' get free?"

Kessler leaned back in his chair, looking thoughtful for a few minutes. His face was clouded, as if he thought of ugly crosses bent at right angles burning through the night. Finally he wiped the crumbs from his beard, then smiled, his gray eyes gleaming.

"Tell me about it."

#

The children were there, just as Minnie had promised, though Kessler hadn't expected to find them circled so tightly around her. He edged closer, past the two cannons and General Nathan Bedford Forrest, whose stone gaze seemed fixed on Minnie. She was magnificent, perched on a park bench, tambourine in hand, draped in a gown that looked as if it had been spun from three bolts of "Confederate fabric." Her voice, rich and unwavering, filled the afternoon air.

From the edge of the crowd, Swing-Lo squinted, adjusting his glasses. He hadn't seen Minnie in her new . . . costume. It shimmered in the sun, a kaleidoscope of bright orange and battle gray. Beside him, Darius nudged his arm, a wide grin splitting his face. The little girls from the jump rope crew, their braids bouncing, were already swaying, some of them mouthing the words to a song Swing-Lo recognized, but only just. He'd never heard it sung this way.

#

I wish I was in the land of cotton,
Old times there are not forgotten;
Look away! Look away!
Look away, Dixie's Land!

The small crowd of bystanders looked appalled, as if they did not know if they should be offended or applaud. Only the children looked at ease. When Minnie's voice rang out with the second verse, the kids joined in, waving little rebel flags.

#

In Dixie's Land where I was born in,
Early on one frosty morning,
Look away! Look away!
Look away, Dixie's Land!

#

Kessler was dumbfounded. He had never heard it sung quite like that, a little odd but it grew on you. The children sang so joyously, and Minnie—she was magnificent, all stars and stripes and rebel orange.

A young man dressed in a jogging suit stared at Kessler, daring him to join in. Another man gripping a briefcase looked embarrassed and shot him a dirty look. Kessler wiped his brow with unsteady hands, keeping his eyes on Minnie. The sun beamed directly above them.

"What is this bullshit?" the young man asked no one in particular. Kessler and Briefcase Man did not answer.

A short boy in glasses spoke up.

"That's Black Power, man. You mean, you didn't know?"

The three men exchanged glances.

#

After a few more performances, word spread about Memphis Minnie and her burgeoning children's choir. Soon, Swing-Lo, Darius, and the spirited Double-Dutch girls were not only her backup singers but also her impromptu dancers, bringing joyous, unrehearsed energy to every stage. The Action News 5 crew showed up to get thirty-second sound bites and soon Memphis Minnie and the Littlest Rebels were all over the Mid-South.

Black and white photos featuring Minnie and her magnificent costume appeared in both dailies simultaneously. *The Commercial*

Appeal and *The Memphis Repeal,* old rivals, competed for exclusive interviews. Even *The Tri-State Defender*, the city's lone independent, got in on the action. They interviewed a few old blues singers who had traveled with Minnie during her youth, the Chitlin Circuit days; one of them turned out to be the father of a woman named Regina.

#

Over the next few weeks, sightings of Confederate flags increased. Soon, cars and trucks sporting the bright orange flags and being driven by black people could be seen all over the South. They were ripping and running, drag racing up and down Riverside Drive and cruising along B.B. King (Third Street). Low riders and big bodies with demon engines transformed into pimped out, custom Dixie rides, thundered past, bass-thumping versions of the old Southern Dixie cry, much to the silent disgust of the bewildered States' Rights and Heritage crowd. Hot boys and old g's in Rebel flag-adorned Cadillacs and chrome were tearing up the Memphis streets.

Ministers and college students, executives and professionals wore "Rebel" buttons and brooches on their lapels and clips on their silk ties. Black women wore "Rebel" bandanas in their hair with panache. Pineapple up-dos, feathered-out pixie cuts and bamboos with rebel flag diamond-studded grills in their teeth, rebel bars on their cheeks.

Later that season, a trendy designer introduced a new line of clothes. The teenagers went wild. Soon sightings of black folks in fashionable Rebel gear became common.

After all the excitement, Minnie got a few gigs down on Beale, even a local car dealer commercial, and when she looked out into the crowd, she saw nothing but rebels. She became so popular with her unique repertoire of blues, spirituals, and Old Dixie, that she started working the convention circuit.

The first time she sang "Dixie" at the Annual Million Black Man, Woman, and Child and N'em March in Atlanta, the strange looks, sidelong glances, and outrage changed to bemused laughter and finally to open joking and acceptance. Minnie even had the R&B band jazz it up a bit with the new 8 Ball & MG remixed version. The nation watched in awe as one million blacks raised their collective voices singing, "I wish I was in the land of cotton, old times there are not forgotten . . ." Of course, the media covered the story and reported the turnout conservatively.

The Rebel flag became so common that the marching bands of historically Black colleges and universities paraded it at homecoming. The drum majors and majorettes at TSU's Aristocrats of Bands really fucked that shit up, bringing the crowds to a frenzy. And after Minnie and the children's version of the Dixie song was sung right after the National Black Anthem in gyms and stadiums, and the flag was flown at family reunions, Juneteenth, and Fourth of July celebrations all across the nation, the historic emblem quietly disappeared from its station atop the State Capitol. There was no ceremony, no notice, no nothing. One day it simply was not there.

Look away, look away, look away, Dixie's land.

Memphis Minnie III

Coded Language

A GUITAR, NOT JUST wood and wire, but a shield, a weapon, a whispered code. "My baby cried just like a child"—not lullaby, but a warning. A body blooming too soon, a future stolen before it could be named. Indigo bottle trees, catching whispers of what couldn't be said aloud. Jim Crow's shadow stretching long, a sundown town in every note. Separate fountains, separate doors, separate lives. The back of the bus, the back of the hand, the weight of knowing your place.

Screams echoing in the slide guitar, a moan for Emmett, a cry for every girl snatched in the night. Violence, not a stranger, but a constant companion. Little boys with eyes too old, learning the language of survival before they learned their ABCs. Masks woven from smiles and downcast gazes, a performance for white folks, a secret language shared in the dark. "Frisco Town," not a destination, but a desperate prayer, a phantom train rattling towards a city of broken promises. A place where back-alley whispers met cold steel and a woman's body became a battleground. A one-way ticket to a stolen future, a whispered name on a clinic door. Lizzie Douglas knew this road, every pothole, every hidden danger.

Her voice, whiskey-soaked and raw, a testament to what she carried. Each note a scar, each chord a battle cry. Hands that picked cotton, hands that strummed defiance, hands that held babies too soon gone. The blues, not just a genre, but a survival kit, filled with coded messages and hidden strength. What she left behind: the innocence of childhood, the luxury of safety, the recognition of her humanity. What she carried: the weight of history, the fire of resistance, the unwavering will to sing her truth, even when no one wanted to hear it. Her music, a map through the minefield of the South, a beacon for those lost in the dark.

But the dark still lingers, the journey continues.

Generations in the Steam

Sit, child.
The silence in this room has roots.
Bring your skinned knees, your heart-splinters
the questions blooming too bright behind your eyes.
You see the lines around my mouth
the way my shoulders curve toward the earth
and maybe you feel a chill.

But lean closer.
Smell the steam rising from this cup?
That's High John, grounded slow, for mastery.
And snakeroot, for truths coiled tight inside.
This isn't the sweet brew of girlhood dreams
nor the sustaining draught of motherhood's long days.

This tea holds the bitterness of hindsight
the sharp clarity of shed illusions.
It teaches what the nettle knows
what the deep-dug mandrake understands
about holding fast when the world pulls.

Drink. Learn the flavor of your own resilience.
The Maiden seeks, the Mother builds

but the Crone . . . the Crone remembers the earth's first name
and harvests power where others see only weeds.
This knowledge doesn't end. It ripens.
Pass the cup.

About the Author

Sheree Renée Thomas is a *New York Times* bestselling, award-winning author, poet, and editor. Her work is inspired by myth, folklore, natural science, music, and Mississippi Delta conjure. She's the author of the Marvel novel *Black Panther: Panther's Rage* (Titan Books, 2022) and of four previous collections: *Mojorhythm* (Third Man Books, 2025), *Nine Bar Blues* (2020), *Sleeping Under the Tree of Life* and *Shotgun Lullabies* (Aqueduct Press, 2016, 2011). She collaborated with Janelle Monáe on "Timebox Altar(ed)" in Monáe's debut fiction collection, *The Memory Librarian and Other Stories of Dirty Computer* (HarperVoyager, 2022).

Sheree's work has appeared in numerous publications, including *The Big Book of Modern Fantasy*; *Sycorax's Daughters*; *Afrofuturo(s)*; *Jalada*; *Memphis Noir*; *Black Panther: Tales of Wakanda*; *Stories for Chip: A Tribute to Samuel R. Delany*; *So Long Been Dreaming: Post-colonial Science Fiction & Fantasy; Luminescent Threads: Connections to Octavia E. Butler*; *Mojo: Conjure Stories*; *Curating the End of the World*; *Ghost Fishing: An Eco-Justice Poetry Anthology*; *The Moment of Change: Feminist Speculative Poetry, Memories & Reflections on Ursula K. Le Guin*; *Hurricane Blues; Fiyah*; *Strange Horizons*; *Obsidian*; *Callaloo*; *Essence*; *Vibe*; *The Washington Post Book World*; *Scientific American*; and *The New York Times.*

Sheree edited the groundbreaking anthologies *Dark Matter: A Century of Speculative Fiction from the African Diaspora* (2000) and *Dark Matter: Reading the Bones* (2004), and coedited *Africa Risen: A New Era of Speculative Fiction* (2022). In 2001, Sheree became the first Black author to receive a World Fantasy Award, an honor eventually earned by all three anthologies, with *Africa Risen* also winning the Locus Award. A two-time Hugo Award Finalist, she served as a 2019 Guest of Honor at the World Fantasy Awards and a 2021 Writer Guest of Honor for Worldcon, where she cohosted the Hugo Awards Ceremony. She was also a 2021 Guest of Honor for WisCon, the world's premiere feminist science fiction convention.

Sheree was honored with the Octavia E. Butler Award and the LA Banks Award. She serves as associate editor of the historic, award-winning Black Arts literary journal, *Obsidian: Literature & Arts in the African Diaspora* (Illinois State University, founded 1975) and is editor of *The Magazine of Fantasy & Science Fiction* (founded 1949).

FRIENDS OF PM

These are indisputably momentous times—the financial system is melting down globally and the Empire is stumbling. Now more than ever there is a vital need for radical ideas.

In the years since its founding—and on a mere shoestring—PM Press has risen to the formidable challenge of publishing and distributing knowledge and entertainment for the struggles ahead. With hundreds of releases to date, we have published an impressive and stimulating array of literature, art, music, politics, and culture. Using every available medium, we've succeeded in connecting those hungry for ideas and information to those putting them into practice.

Friends of PM allows you to directly help impact, amplify, and revitalize the discourse and actions of radical writers, filmmakers, and artists. It provides us with a stable foundation from which we can build upon our early successes and provides a much-needed subsidy for the materials that can't necessarily pay their own way. You can help make that happen—and receive every new title automatically delivered to your door once a month—by joining as a Friend of PM Press. And, we'll throw in a free T-shirt when you sign up.

Here are your options:

- $30 a month: Get all books and pamphlets plus 50% discount on all webstore purchases
- $40 a month: Get all PM Press releases (including CDs and DVDs) plus 50% discount on all webstore purchases
- $100 a month: Superstar—Everything plus PM merchandise, free downloads, and 50% discount on all webstore purchases

For those who can't afford $30 or more a month, we have Sustainer Rates at $15, $10, and $5. Sustainers get a free PM Press T-shirt and a 50% discount on all purchases from our website.

Your Visa or Mastercard will be billed once a month, until you tell us to stop. Or until our efforts succeed in bringing the revolution around. Or the financial meltdown of Capital makes plastic redundant. Whichever comes first.

PM Press is an independent, radical publisher of critically necessary books for our tumultuous times. Our aim is to deliver bold political ideas and vital stories to all walks of life and arm the dreamers to demand the impossible. Founded in 2007 by a small group of people with decades of publishing, media, and organizing experience, we have sold millions of copies of our books, most often one at a time, face to face. We're old enough to know what we're doing and young enough to know what's at stake. Join us to create a better world.

PM Press
PO Box 23912
Oakland, CA 94623
info@pmpress.org

PM Press in Europe
europe@pmpress.org
www.pmpress.org.uk

Fire on the Mountain

Terry Bisson
Introduction by Mumia Abu-Jamal
ISBN: 978-1-60486-087-0
208 pages • 5 x 8 • $18.95

It's 1959 in socialist Virginia. The Deep South is an independent Black nation called Nova Africa. The second Mars expedition is about to touch down on the red planet. And a pregnant scientist is climbing the Blue Ridge in search of her great-great grandfather, a teenage slave who fought with John Brown and Harriet Tubman's guerrilla army.

Long unavailable in the U.S., published in France as *Nova Africa*, *Fire on the Mountain* is the story of what might have happened if John Brown's raid on Harper's Ferry had succeeded—and the Civil War had been started not by the slave owners but the abolitionists.

"History revisioned, turned inside out . . . Bisson's wild and wonderful imagination has taken some strange turns to arrive at such a destination."
—Madison Smartt Bell, Anisfield-Wolf Award winner and author of *Devil's Dream*

TERRY BISSON
THE LEFT LEFT BEHIND
KIM STANLEY ROBINSON
THE LUCKY STRIKE
ELEANOR ARNASON
MAMMOTHS OF THE GREAT PLAINS
GARY PHILLIPS
THE UNDERBELLY
MICHAEL MOORCOCK
MODEM TIMES 2.0
URSULA K. LE GUIN
THE WILD GIRLS
CORY DOCTOROW
THE GREAT BIG BEAUTIFUL TOMORROW
RUDY RUCKER
SURFING THE GNARL
NALO HOPKINSON
REPORT FROM PLANET MIDNIGHT
KEN MACLEOD
THE HUMAN FRONT
JOHN SHIRLEY
NEW TABOOS
KAREN JOY FOWLER
THE SCIENCE OF HERSELF
NORMAN SPINRAD
RAISING HELL
PAUL KRASSNER
PATTY HEARST & THE TWINKIE MURDERS: A TALE OF TWO TRIALS
MARGE PIERCY
MY LIFE, MY BODY
CARTER SCHOLZ
GYPSY

OUTSPOKEN AUTHORS

The Outspoken and the Incendiary
Interviews with Radical Speculative Fiction Writers

Terry Bisson
Foreword by Jonathan Lethem
Introduction by Nisi Shawl
Afterword by Nalo Hopkinson
Elegies by Rudy Rucker and Peter Coyote
ISBN: 979-8-88744-121-4
416 pages • 6 x 9 • $24.95

For more than a decade, radical science fiction author and activist journalist Terry Bisson interviewed some of the most provocative and outspoken authors of the twentieth and twenty-first centuries. Anarchism, sexuality, creativity, and the future of humanity itself—no topic was taboo. Bisson's prankster spirit also shone through as he quizzed his subjects about what cars they drove, played free association games, and created an atmosphere of two old friends having intimate late-night chats. Collected from PM Press's award-winning Outspoken Authors series for the first time, *The Outspoken and the Incendiary* showcases insightful and long-form explorations into the lives and minds of some of today's most politically charged fiction writers.

Words and Thoughts By: Eleanor Arnason, Terry Bisson, Michael Blumlein, John Crowley, Samuel R. Delany, Cory Doctorow, Meg Elison, Karen Joy Fowler, Eileen Gunn, Elizabeth Hand, Cara Hoffman, Nalo Hopkinson, James Patrick Kelly, John Kessel, Paul Krassner, Joe R. Lansdale, Jonathan Lethem, Ursula K. Le Guin, Ken MacLeod, Nick Mamatas, Michael Moorcock, Paul Park, Gary Phillips, Marge Piercy, Rachel Pollack, Rudy Rucker, Kim Stanley Robinson, Carter Scholz, Nisi Shawl, John Shirley, Vandana Singh, and Norman Spinrad, with additional new contributions by Nalo Hopkinson, Jonathan Lethem, Nisi Shawl, Peter Coyote, and Rudy Rucker.

SHEREE RENÉE THOMAS

Twice nominated for the Hugo Award,
winner of Locus Award and Octavia E. Butler Award,
and three-time winner of the World Fantasy Award

"If you like Octavia Butler's *Parable* duology, Alice Walker's *The Temple of My Familiar*, or the poetry of Sonia Sanchez, you'll love this collection."
—Mara Mathews of Quail Ridge Books

"Sheree R. Thomas is a hoodoo conjure woman. Thomas calls on the ancestors, the spirits, and our natural Mississippi mud/blood history to talk to the future."
—Andrea Hairston, author of *Archangels of Funk*

"When great soul meets great work, what you get is a thing of wonder."
—Arthur Flowers, NEA fellow and author of *The Hoodoo Book of Flowers: The Great Black Book of Generations*

"Thomas's skill with poetry and prose is remarkable."
—*Publishers Weekly*

"A master of the craft and a true literary alchemist, Thomas blends the joys and sorrows of action, diaspora, spirituality, culture, and love into absolute gold."
—Daniel José Older, *New York Times* bestselling author

"A whirlpool of poem and story. . . . Thomas's skill with poetry and prose is remarkable, and even the shortest poems in this volume contain ideas and images that will linger in the reader's mind."
—Tyehimba Jess, Pulitzer Prize winner,
author of *Olio* and *Leadbelly*

"Sheree Renée Thomas is an award-winning writer . . . a storyteller . . . who has expanded the territory, as well as the audience for science fiction, speculative fiction, and fantasy."
—George Larrimore, PBS

"Thomas is a griot for the 21st century."
—WRAL

PM PRESS OUTSPOKEN AUTHORS SERIES

1. *The Left Left Behind*
   Terry Bisson
2. *The Lucky Strike*
   Kim Stanley Robinson
3. *The Underbelly*
   Gary Phillips
4. *Mammoths of the Great Plains*
   Eleanor Arnason
5. *Modem Times 2.0*
   Michael Moorcock
6. *The Wild Girls*
   Ursula K. Le Guin
7. *Surfing the Gnarl*
   Rudy Rucker
8. *The Great Big Beautiful Tomorrow*
   Cory Doctorow
9. *Report from Planet Midnight*
   Nalo Hopkinson
10. *The Human Front*
    Ken MacLeod
11. *New Taboos*
    John Shirley
12. *The Science of Herself*
    Karen Joy Fowler
13. *Raising Hell*
    Norman Spinrad
14. *Patty Hearst & The Twinkie Murders: A Tale of Two Trials*
    Paul Krassner
15. *My Life, My Body*
    Marge Piercy
16. *Gypsy*
    Carter Scholz
17. *Miracles Ain't What They Used to Be*
    Joe R. Lansdale
18. *Fire.*
    Elizabeth Hand
19. *Totalitopia*
    John Crowley
20. *The Atheist in the Attic*
    Samuel R. Delany
21. *Thoreau's Microscope*
    Michael Blumlein
22. *The Beatrix Gates*
    Rachel Pollack
23. *A City Made of Words*
    Paul Park
24. *Talk like a Man*
    Nisi Shawl
25. *Big Girl*
    Meg Elison
26. *The Planetbreaker's Son*
    Nick Mamatas
27. *The First Law of Thermodynamics*
    James Patrick Kelly
28. *Utopias of the Third Kind*
    Vandana Singh
29. *Night Shift*
    Eileen Gunn
30. *The Collapsing Frontier*
    Jonathan Lethem

31. *The Presidential Papers*
John Kessel

32. *The Last Coward on Earth*
Cara Hoffman

33. *Not What I Intended*
Nancy Kress

34. *She Is Here*
Nicola Griffith

35. *Veni Vidi Venti*
Ian Shoales

36. *The Tongue I Dream In*
Sheree Renée Thomas

37. *Machine Elves Descending*
John King

38. *FLUME*
Brian Evenson

39. *The History of the Decline and Fall of the Galactic Empire*
Toh EnJoe